DOVER·THRIFT·EDITIONS

Othello

WILLIAM SHAKESPEARE

DOVER PUBLICATIONS, INC.
Mineola, New York

DOVER THRIFT EDITIONS

GENERAL EDITOR: STANLEY APPELBAUM
EDITOR OF THIS VOLUME: CANDACE WARD

Theatrical Rights

This Dover Thrift Edition may be used in its entirety, in adaptation or in any other way for theatrical productions, professional and amateur, in the United States, without fee, permission or acknowledgment. (This may not apply outside of the United States, as copyright conditions may vary.)

Bibliographical Note

This Dover edition, first published in 1996, contains the unabridged text of *Othello* as published in Volume XVI of *The Caxton Edition of the Complete Works of William Shakespeare*, Caxton Publishing Company, London, n.d. The Note was prepared specially for this edition, and explanatory footnotes from the Caxton edition have been supplemented and revised.

Library of Congress Cataloging-in-Publication Data

Shakespeare, William, 1564–1616.
    Othello / William Shakespeare.
        p.   cm. — (Dover thrift editions)
    ISBN 0-486-29097-2 (pbk.)
    I. Title.   II. Series.
PR2829.A1   1996
822.3'3 — dc20   96-1263
                                                      CIP

Manufactured in the United States of America
Dover Publications, Inc., 31 East 2nd Street, Mineola, N.Y. 11501

Note

SINCE ITS FIRST performance in 1604, *Othello* has proved one of Shakespeare's most enduring tragedies. The play, set against the backdrop of the Venetian–Turkish wars, features one of Shakespeare's most compelling villains, Iago. Ostensibly driven by a desire for revenge, Iago plots and schemes to bring about Othello's fall. But his malignancy appears incommensurate to the wrongs he claims Othello has done him. Indeed, Iago uses the fact that he was passed over for promotion to enlist Roderigo's aid rather than to offer a legitimate motive for his behavior. Even his offhand aside reporting a rumor that Othello slept with his wife seems implausible, and all we have is Iago's simple statement: "I hate the Moor.".

Othello provides the perfect foil for Iago and the latter's description illustrates his contempt of the tragic hero. "The Moor is of a free and open nature," Iago tells us, "And will as tenderly be led by the nose / As asses are." Iago's comparison of Othello to an ass is one of many animal images he applies to his enemy. Othello is an "old black ram," a beast, a "Barbary horse." Sprung from Iago's hatred, these images of blackness and brutishness point up Othello's tenuous position in Venetian society. And Othello's reluctant but complete conviction of Desdemona's infidelity speaks of an insecurity born of his marginalized position.

For Desdemona, Othello's "wondrous pitiful" story strikes a sympathetic chord that arouses first her compassion, then her passion. Under Iago's direction, however, the lovers appear mere pawns, as easily manipulated as the less heroic characters in the play. And we are caught in Iago's plottings too, for despite our privileged access to his plans, we never learn "Why he hath thus ensnared [Othello's] soul and body." All we are left with, in the end, are Iago's last words: "What you know, you know."

Dramatis Personæ

DUKE OF VENICE.
BRABANTIO, a senator.
Other Senators.
GRATIANO, brother to Brabantio.
LODOVICO, kinsman to Brabantio.
OTHELLO, a noble Moor in the service of the Venetian state.
CASSIO, his lieutenant.
IAGO, his ancient.
RODERIGO, a Venetian gentleman.
MONTANO, Othello's predecessor in the government of Cyprus.
Clown, servant to Othello.

DESDEMONA, daughter to Brabantio and wife to Othello.
EMILIA, wife to Iago.
BIANCA, mistress to Cassio.

Sailor, Messenger, Herald, Officers, Gentlemen, Musicians, and
    Attendants.

SCENE: *Venice: a seaport in Cyprus*

ACT I.

SCENE I. *Venice. A Street.*

Enter RODERIGO *and* IAGO

ROD.　Tush, never tell me;[1] I take it much unkindly
　　That thou, Iago, who hast had my purse
　　As if the strings were thine, shouldst know of this.
IAGO.　'Sblood, but you will not hear me:
　　If ever I did dream of such a matter,
　　Abhor me.
ROD.　Thou told'st me thou didst hold him in thy hate.
IAGO.　Despise me, if I do not. Three great ones of the city,
　　In personal suit to make me his lieutenant,
　　Off-capp'd to[2] him: and, by the faith of man,
　　I know my price, I am worth no worse a place:
　　But he, as loving his own pride and purposes,
　　Evades them, with a bombast circumstance
　　Horribly stuff'd with epithets of war;
　　And, in conclusion,
　　Nonsuits[3] my mediators; for, "Certes," says he,
　　"I have already chose my officer."
　　And what was he?
　　Forsooth, a great arithmetician,
　　One Michael Cassio, a Florentine,
　　A fellow almost damn'd in a fair wife;
　　That never set a squadron in the field,
　　Nor the division of a battle knows
　　More than a spinster; unless the bookish theoric,
　　Wherein the toged[4] consuls can propose

---

1. *Tush . . . me*] The scene opens in the middle of a conversation about Othello's elopement with Desdemona.
2. *Off-capp'd to*] Stood cap in hand soliciting.
3. *Nonsuits*] To disappoint in a suit, not to comply with.
4. *toged*] wearing the "toga," the uniform of civil officers of state as opposed to military officers.

As masterly as he: mere prattle without practice
Is all his soldiership. But he, sir, had the election:
And I, of whom his eyes had seen the proof
At Rhodes, at Cyprus, and on other grounds
Christian and heathen, must be be-lee'd[5] and calm'd
By debitor and creditor: this counter-caster,[6]
He, in good time, must his lieutenant be,
And I — God bless the mark! — his Moorship's ancient.[7]

ROD. By heaven, I rather would have been his hangman.

IAGO. Why, there 's no remedy; 't is the curse of service,
Preferment goes by letter and affection,
And not by old gradation, where each second
Stood heir to the first. Now, sir, be judge yourself
Whether I in any just term am affined[8]
To love the Moor.

ROD.   I would not follow him then.

IAGO. O, sir, content you;
I follow him to serve my turn upon him:
We cannot all be masters, nor all masters
Cannot be truly follow'd. You shall mark
Many a duteous and knee-crooking knave,
That doting on his own obsequious bondage
Wears out his time, much like his master's ass,
For nought but provender,[9] and when he 's old, cashier'd:
Whip me such honest knaves. Others there are
Who, trimm'd in forms and visages of duty,
Keep yet their hearts attending on themselves,
And throwing but shows of service on their lords
Do well thrive by them, and when they have lined their coats
Do themselves homage: these fellows have some soul,
And such a one do I profess myself.
For, sir,
It is as sure as you are Roderigo,
Were I the Moor, I would not be Iago:
In following him, I follow but myself;
Heaven is my judge, not I for love and duty,
But seeming so, for my peculiar end:
For when my outward action doth demonstrate

---

5. *be-lee'd*] under the lee of another, out of the way of the wind, and so becalmed (as of a ship).
6. *counter-caster*] one who casts up counters; an old method of accountancy.
7. *ancient*] a colloquial mispronunciation of "ensign."
8. *affined*] bound by close terms of affinity, such as kin- or friendship.
9. *provender*] dry food for animals.

The native act and figure of my heart
In compliment extern,[10] 't is not long after
But I will wear my heart upon my sleeve
For daws to peck at: I am not what I am.

ROD.   What a full fortune does the thick-lips owe,
     If he can carry 't thus!

IAGO.   Call up her father,[11]
     Rouse him: make after him, poison his delight,
     Proclaim him in the streets; incense her kinsmen,
     And, though he in a fertile climate dwell,
     Plague him with flies: though that his joy be joy,
     Yet throw such changes of vexation on 't
     As it may lose some colour.

ROD.   Here is her father's house; I 'll call aloud.

IAGO.   Do; with like timorous accent and dire yell
     As when, by night and negligence, the fire
     Is spied in populous cities.

ROD.   What, ho, Brabantio! Signior Brabantio, ho!

IAGO.   Awake! what, ho, Brabantio! thieves! thieves! thieves!
     Look to your house, your daughter and your bags!
     Thieves! thieves!

BRABANTIO *appears above, at a window*

BRA.   What is the reason of this terrible summons?
     What is the matter there?

ROD.   Signior, is all your family within?

IAGO.   Are your doors lock'd?

BRA.   Why, wherefore ask you this?

IAGO.   'Zounds, sir, you're robb'd; for shame, put on your gown;
     Your heart is burst, you have lost half your soul;
     Even now, now, very now, an old black ram — *describing*
     Is tupping your white ewe. Arise, arise; *Othello.*
     Awake the snorting citizens with the bell,
     Or else the devil will make a grandsire of you:
     Arise, I say.

BRA.   What, have you lost your wits?

ROD.   Most reverend signior, do you know my voice?

BRA.   Not I: what are you?

ROD.   My name is Roderigo.

BRA.   The worser welcome:

---

10. *In compliment extern*] In external etiquette or behaviour.
11. *her father*] i. e., Desdemona's father.

    I have charged thee not to haunt about my doors:
    In honest plainness thou hast heard me say
    My daughter is not for thee; and now, in madness,
    Being full of supper and distempering draughts,
    Upon malicious bravery, dost thou come
    To start my quiet.
ROD.   Sir, sir, sir, —
BRA.   But thou must needs be sure
    My spirit and my place have in them power
    To make this bitter to thee.
ROD.   Patience, good sir.
BRA.   What tell'st thou me of robbing? this is Venice;
    My house is not a grange.
ROD.   Most grave Brabantio,
    In simple and pure soul I come to you.
IAGO.   'Zounds, sir, you are one of those that will not serve God, if the
    devil bid you. Because we come to do you service and you think
    we are ruffians, you 'll have your daughter covered with a Bar-
    bary horse; you 'll have your nephews[12] neigh to you; you 'll have
    coursers for cousins, and gennets for germans.[13]
BRA.   What profane wretch art thou?
IAGO.   I am one, sir, that comes to tell you your daughter and the Moor
    are now making the beast with two backs.
BRA.   Thou art a villain.
IAGO.   You are — a senator.
BRA.   This thou shalt answer; I know thee, Roderigo.
ROD.   Sir, I will answer any thing. But, I beseech you,
    If 't be your pleasure and most wise consent,
    As partly I find it is, that your fair daughter,
    At this odd-even and dull watch o' the night,
    Transported with no worse nor better guard
    But with a knave of common hire, a gondolier,
    To the gross clasps of a lascivious Moor, —
    If this be known to you, and your allowance,[14]
    We then have done you bold and saucy wrongs;
    But if you know not this, my manners tell me
    We have your wrong rebuke. Do not believe
    That, from the sense of all civility,
    I thus would play and trifle with your reverence:
    Your daughter, if you have not given her leave,

---

12. *nephews*] grandsons.
13. *gennets for germans*] (small Spanish) horses for kinsmen.
14. *allowance*] authorization, permission.

I say again, hath made a gross revolt,
Tying her duty, beauty, wit and fortunes,
In an extravagant and wheeling stranger
Of here and every where. Straight satisfy yourself:
If she be in her chamber or your house,
Let loose on me the justice of the state
For thus deluding you.

BRA.   Strike on the tinder, ho!
Give me a taper! call up all my people!
This accident is not unlike my dream:
Belief of it oppresses me already.
Light, I say! light!   [*Exit above.*]

IAGO.   Farewell; for I must leave you:
It seems not meet, nor wholesome to my place,
To be produced — as, if I stay, I shall —
Against the Moor: for I do know, the state,
However this may gall him with some check,[15]
Cannot with safety cast[16] him; for he 's embark'd
With such loud reason to the Cyprus wars,
Which even now stand in act, that, for their souls,
Another of his fathom[17] they have none
To lead their business: in which regard,
Though I do hate him as I do hell pains,
Yet for necessity of present life,
I must show out a flag and sign of love,
Which is indeed but sign. That you shall surely find him,
Lead to the Sagittary[18] the raised search;
And there will I be with him. So farewell.   [*Exit.*]

Enter, below, BRABANTIO, *in his night-gown, and* Servants *with torches*

BRA.   It is too true an evil: gone she is;
And what 's to come of my despised time
Is nought but bitterness. Now, Roderigo,
Where didst thou see her? O unhappy girl!
With the Moor, say'st thou? Who would be a father!
How didst thou know 't was she? O, she deceives me
Past thought! What said she to you? Get more tapers.
Raise all my kindred. Are they married, think you?

---

15. *check*] rebuke.
16. *cast*] dismiss, reject.
17. *fathom*] capacity.
18. *the Sagittary*] probably intended for the name of a well-known inn.

ROD. Truly, I think they are.

BRA. O heaven! How got she out? O treason of the blood!
Fathers, from hence trust not your daughters' minds
By what you see them act. Is there not charms
By which the property of youth and maidhood
May be abused? Have you not read, Roderigo,
Of some such thing?

ROD.   Yes, sir, I have indeed.

BRA. Call up my brother. O, would you had had her!
Some one way, some another. Do you know
Where we may apprehend her and the Moor?

ROD. I think I can discover him, if you please
To get good guard and go along with me.

BRA. Pray you, lead on. At every house I 'll call;
I may command at most. Get weapons, ho!
And raise some special officers of night.
On, good Roderigo; I 'll deserve your pains.   [*Exeunt.*]

SCENE II. *Another Street.*

Enter OTHELLO, IAGO, *and* Attendants *with torches*

IAGO. Though in the trade of war I have slain men,
Yet do I hold it very stuff o' the conscience
To do no contrived murder: I lack iniquity
Sometimes to do me service: nine or ten times
I had thought to have yerk'd[1] him here under the ribs.

OTH. 'T is better as it is.

IAGO.   Nay, but he prated
And spoke such scurvy and provoking terms
Against your honour,
That, with the little godliness I have,
I did full hard forbear him. But I pray you, sir,
Are you fast married? Be assured of this,
That the magnifico is much beloved,
And hath in his effect a voice potential
As double as the duke's: he will divorce you,
Or put upon you what restraint and grievance

---

1. *yerk'd*] jerked; to have given a thrust with a sudden and quick motion.

     The law, with all his might to enforce it on,
     Will give him cable.[2]

OTH.   Let him do his spite:
     My services, which I have done the signiory,
     Shall out-tongue his complaints. 'T is yet to know —
     Which, when I know that boasting is an honour,
     I shall promulgate — I fetch my life and being
     From men of royal siege, and my demerits
     May speak unbonneted to as proud a fortune
     As this that I have reach'd: for know, Iago,
     But that I love the gentle Desdemona,
     I would not my unhoused free condition
     Put into circumscription and confine
     For the sea's worth. But, look! what lights come yond?

IAGO.   Those are the raised father and his friends:
     You were best go in.

OTH.   Not I; I must be found:
     My parts, my title and my perfect soul,
     Shall manifest me rightly. Is it they?

IAGO.   By Janus, I think no.

Enter CASSIO, *and certain* Officers *with torches*

OTH.   The servants of the duke, and my lieutenant.
     The goodness of the night upon you, friends!
     What is the news?

CAS.   The duke does greet you, general,
     And he requires your haste-post-haste appearance,
     Even on the instant.

OTH.   What is the matter, think you?

CAS.   Something from Cyprus, as I may divine:
     It is a business of some heat: the galleys
     Have sent a dozen sequent[3] messengers
     This very night at one another's heels;
     And many of the consuls, raised and met,
     Are at the duke's already: you have been hotly call'd for;
     When, being not at your lodging to be found,
     The senate hath sent about three several quests[4]
     To search you out.

OTH.   'T is well I am found by you.

---

2. *cable*] full means or opportunity.

3. *sequent*] following one another, one after the other.

4. *quests*] search parties.

    I will but spend a word here in the house,
    And go with you.   [*Exit.*]
CAS.   Ancient, what makes he here?
IAGO.   Faith, he to-night hath boarded a land carack:[5]
    If it prove lawful prize, he 's made for ever.
CAS.   I do not understand.
IAGO.   He 's married.
CAS.   To who?

Re-enter OTHELLO

IAGO.   Marry, to — Come, captain, will you go?
OTH.   Have with you.[6]
CAS.   Here comes another troop to seek for you.
IAGO.   It is Brabantio: general, be advised;
    He comes to bad intent.

Enter BRABANTIO, RODERIGO, *and* Officers *with torches and weapons*

OTH.   Holla! stand there!
ROD.   Signior, it is the Moor.
BRA.   Down with him, thief!
                            [*They draw on both sides.*]
IAGO.   You, Roderigo! come, sir, I am for you.
OTH.   Keep up your bright swords, for the dew will rust them.
    Good signior, you shall more command with years
    Than with your weapons.
BRA.   O thou foul thief, where hast thou stow'd my daughter?
    Damn'd as thou art, thou hast enchanted her;
    For I 'll refer me to all things of sense,
    If she in chains of magic were not bound,
    Whether a maid so tender, fair and happy,
    So opposite to marriage that she shunn'd
    The wealthy curled darlings of our nation,
    Would ever have, to incur a general mock,
    Run from her guardage[7] to the sooty bosom
    Of such a thing as thou, to fear, not to delight.
    Judge me the world, if 't is not gross in sense
    That thou hast practised on her with foul charms,
    Abused her delicate youth with drugs or minerals
    That weaken motion: I 'll have 't disputed on;

---

5. *a land carack*] a ship of great burden on land.
6. *Have with you*] I am quite ready.
7. *guardage*] guardianship.

'T is probable, and palpable to thinking.
I therefore apprehend and do attach[8] thee
For an abuser of the world, a practiser
Of arts inhibited and out of warrant.[9]
Lay hold upon him: if he do resist,
Subdue him at his peril.

OTH.   Hold your hands,
Both you of my inclining and the rest:
Were it my cue to fight, I should have known it
Without a prompter. Where will you that I go
To answer this your charge?

BRA.   To prison, till fit time
Of law and course of direct session
Call thee to answer.

OTH.   What if I do obey?
How may the duke be therewith satisfied,
Whose messengers are here about my side,
Upon some present business of the state
To bring me to him?

FIRST OFF.   'T is true, most worthy signior;
The duke's in council, and your noble self,
I am sure, is sent for.

BRA.   How! the duke in council!
In this time of the night! Bring him away:
Mine's not an idle cause: the duke himself,
Or any of my brothers of the state,
Cannot but feel this wrong as 't were their own;
For if such actions may have passage free,
Bond-slaves and pagans shall our statesmen be.   [*Exeunt.*]

SCENE III. *A Council-Chamber.*

The Duke *and* Senators *sitting at a table;* Officers *attending*

DUKE.   There is no composition[1] in these news
That gives them credit.

FIRST SEN.   Indeed they are disproportion'd;
My letters say a hundred and seven galleys.

---

8. *attach*] arrest.
9. *inhibited . . . warrant*] prohibited and unauthorised.
1. *composition*] consistency, coherence.

DUKE.　And mine, a hundred and forty.

SEC. SEN.　　　　　　　　　　　　　And mine, two hundred:
    But though they jump not on a just account, — [2]
    As in these cases, where the aim reports,
    'T is oft with difference, — yet do they all confirm
    A Turkish fleet, and bearing up to Cyprus.

DUKE.　Nay, it is possible enough to judgement:
    I do not so secure me in the error,
    But the main article I do approve[3]
    In fearful sense.

SAILOR.　[*Within*] What, ho! what, ho! what, ho!

FIRST OFF.　A messenger from the galleys.

Enter Sailor

DUKE.　　　　　　　　　　　　　Now, what's the business?

SAIL.　The Turkish preparation[4] makes for Rhodes;
    So was I bid report here to the state
    By Signior Angelo.

DUKE.　How say you by this change?

FIRST SEN.　　　　　　　　　　　This cannot be,
    By no assay[5] of reason: 't is a pageant
    To keep us in false gaze. When we consider
    The importancy of Cyprus to the Turk,
    And let ourselves again but understand
    That as it more concerns the Turk than Rhodes,
    So may he with more facile question bear it,[6]
    For that it stands not in such warlike brace,
    But altogether lacks the abilities
    That Rhodes is dress'd in: if we make thought of this,
    We must not think the Turk is so unskilful
    To leave that latest which concerns him first,
    Neglecting an attempt of ease and gain,
    To wake and wage[7] a danger profitless.

DUKE.　Nay, in all confidence, he 's not for Rhodes.

FIRST OFF.　Here is more news.

---

2. *jump not . . . account*] agree not in an exact estimate.
3. *approve*] believe, give credit to.
4. *preparation*] force ready for action.
5. *assay*] test.
6. *with . . . bear it*] with less opposition contest it.
7. *wake and wage*] excite and challenge.

Enter a Messenger

MESS.   The Ottomites, reverend and gracious,
        Steering with due course toward the isle of Rhodes,
        Have there injointed them[8] with an after fleet.
FIRST SEN.   Ay, so I thought. How many, as you guess?
MESS.   Of thirty sail: and now they do re-stem[9]
        Their backward course, bearing with frank appearance
        Their purposes toward Cyprus. Signior Montano,
        Your trusty and most valiant servitor,
        With his free duty recommends you thus,
        And prays you to believe him.
DUKE.   'T is certain then for Cyprus.
        Marcus Luccicos, is not he in town?
FIRST SEN.   He 's now in Florence.
DUKE.   Write from us to him; post-post-haste dispatch.
FIRST SEN.   Here comes Brabantio and the valiant Moor.

Enter BRABANTIO, OTHELLO, IAGO, RODERIGO, *and* Officers

DUKE.   Valiant Othello, we must straight employ you
        Against the general enemy Ottoman.
        [*To* BRABANTIO] I did not see you; welcome, gentle signior;
        We lack'd your counsel and your help to-night.
BRA.   So did I yours. Good your grace, pardon me;
        Neither my place nor aught I heard of business
        Hath raised me from my bed, nor doth the general care
        Take hold on me; for my particular grief
        Is of so flood-gate and o'erbearing nature
        That it engluts and swallows other sorrows,
        And it is still itself.
DUKE.   Why, what's the matter?
BRA.   My daughter! O, my daughter!
ALL.   Dead?
BRA.   Ay, to me;
        She is abused, stol'n from me and corrupted
        By spells and medicines bought of mountebanks;
        For nature so preposterously to err,
        Being not deficient, blind, or lame of sense,

---

8. *injointed them*] joined their forces, combined.
9. *re-stem*] retrace.

Sans[10] witchcraft could not.

DUKE.   Whoe'er he be that in this foul proceeding
Hath thus beguiled your daughter of herself
And you of her, the bloody book of law
You shall yourself read in the bitter letter
After your own sense, yea, though our proper son
Stood in your action.

BRA.   Humbly I thank your grace.
Here is the man, this Moor; whom now, it seems,
Your special mandate for the state-affairs
Hath hither brought.

ALL.   We are very sorry for 't.

DUKE.   [*To* OTHELLO] What in your own part can you say to this?

BRA.   Nothing, but this is so.

OTH.   Most potent, grave, and reverend signiors,
My very noble and approved good masters,
That I have ta'en away this old man's daughter
It is most true; true, I have married her:
The very head and front of my offending
Hath this extent, no more. Rude am I in my speech,
And little blest with the soft phrase of peace;
For since these arms of mine had seven years' pith,[11]
Till now some nine moons wasted, they have used
Their dearest action in the tented field;
And little of this great world can I speak,
More than pertains to feats of broil and battle;
And therefore little shall I grace my cause
In speaking for myself. Yet, by your gracious patience,
I will a round[12] unvarnish'd tale deliver
Of my whole course of love; what drugs, what charms,
What conjuration and what mighty magic —
For such proceeding I am charged withal —
I won his daughter.

BRA.   A maiden never bold;
Of spirit so still and quiet that her motion
Blush'd at herself; and she — in spite of nature,
Of years, of country, credit, every thing —
To fall in love with what she fear'd to look on!
It is a judgement maim'd and most imperfect,
That will confess perfection so could err

---

10. *Sans*] Without.
11. *pith*] strength, force.
12. *round*] plain, direct.

Against all rules of nature; and must be driven
To find out practices of cunning hell,
Why this should be. I therefore vouch again,
That with some mixtures powerful o'er the blood,
Or with some dram conjured to this effect,
He wrought upon her.
DUKE.   To vouch this, is no proof,
Without more certain and more overt test
Than these thin habits and poor likelihoods
Of modern[13] seeming do prefer against him.
FIRST SEN.   But, Othello, speak:
Did you by indirect and forced courses
Subdue and poison this young maid's affections?
Or came it by request, and such fair question
As soul to soul affordeth?
OTH.   I do beseech you,
Send for the lady to the Sagittary,
And let her speak of me before her father:
If you do find me foul in her report,
The trust, the office I do hold of you,
Not only take away, but let your sentence
Even fall upon my life.
DUKE.   Fetch Desdemona hither.
OTH.   Ancient, conduct them; you best know the place.

> [*Exeunt* IAGO *and* Attendants.]

And till she come, as truly as to heaven
I do confess the vices of my blood,
So justly to your grave ears I 'll present
How I did thrive in this fair lady's love
And she in mine.
DUKE.   Say it, Othello.
OTH.   Her father loved me, oft invited me,
Still question'd me the story of my life
From year to year, the battles, sieges, fortunes,
That I have pass'd.
I ran it through, even from my boyish days
To the very moment that he bade me tell it:
Wherein I spake of most disastrous chances,
Of moving accidents by flood and field,
Of hair-breadth 'scapes i' the imminent deadly breach,
Of being taken by the insolent foe,
And sold to slavery, of my redemption thence,

---

13. *modern*] commonplace, trivial.

And portance in my travels' history:
Wherein of antres[14] vast and deserts idle,
Rough quarries, rocks, and hills whose heads touch heaven,
It was my hint[15] to speak, — such was the process;
And of the Cannibals that each other eat,
The Anthropophagi, and men whose heads
Do grow beneath their shoulders. This to hear
Would Desdemona seriously incline:
But still the house-affairs would draw her thence;
Which ever as she could with haste dispatch,
She 'ld come again, and with a greedy ear
Devour up my discourse: which I observing,
Took once a pliant hour, and found good means
To draw from her a prayer of earnest heart
That I would all my pilgrimage dilate,[16]
Whereof by parcels she had something heard,
But not intentively:[17] I did consent,
And often did beguile her of her tears
When I did speak of some distressful stroke
That my youth suffer'd. My story being done,
She gave me for my pains a world of sighs:
She swore, in faith, 't was strange, 't was passing strange;
'T was pitiful, 't was wondrous pitiful:
She wish'd she had not heard it, yet she wish'd
That heaven had made her such a man: she thank'd me,
And bade me, if I had a friend that loved her,
I should but teach him how to tell my story,
And that would woo her. Upon this hint I spake:
She loved me for the dangers I had pass'd,
And I loved her that she did pity them.
This only is the witchcraft I have used.
Here comes the lady; let her witness it.

Enter DESDEMONA, IAGO, *and* Attendants

DUKE.   I think this tale would win my daughter too.
Good Brabantio,
Take up this mangled matter at the best:
Men do their broken weapons rather use

---

14. *antres*] caves or caverns.
15. *hint*] occasion.
16. *dilate*] relate in full.
17. *intentively*] with full attention, intently.

    Than their bare hands.

BRA.   I pray you, hear her speak:
    If she confess that she was half the wooer,
    Destruction on my head, if my bad blame
    Light on the man! Come hither, gentle mistress:
    Do you perceive in all this noble company
    Where most you owe obedience?

DES.   My noble father,
    I do perceive here a divided duty:
    To you I am bound for life and education;
    My life and education both do learn me
    How to respect you; you are the lord of duty,
    I am hitherto your daughter: but here 's my husband,
    And so much duty as my mother show'd
    To you, preferring you before her father,
    So much I challenge that I may profess
    Due to the Moor my lord.

BRA.   God be with you! I have done.
    Please it your grace, on to the state-affairs:
    I had rather to adopt a child than get it.
    Come hither, Moor:
    I here do give thee that with all my heart,
    Which, but thou hast already, with all my heart
    I would keep from thee. For your sake, jewel,
    I am glad at soul I have no other child;
    For thy escape[18] would teach me tyranny,
    To hang clogs[19] on them. I have done, my lord.

DUKE.   Let me speak like yourself, and lay a sentence
    Which, as a grise[20] or step, may help these lovers
    Into your favour.
    When remedies are past, the griefs are ended
    By seeing the worst, which late on hopes depended.
    To mourn a mischief that is past and gone
    Is the next way to draw new mischief on.
    What cannot be preserved when fortune takes,
    Patience her injury a mockery makes.
    The robb'd that smiles steals something from the thief;
    He robs himself that spends a bootless grief.

BRA.   So let the Turk of Cyprus us beguile;
    We lose it not so long as we can smile.

---

18. *escape*] escapade.
19. *clogs*] anything hung upon an animal to hinder motion.
20. *grise*] step.

He bears the sentence well, that nothing bears
But the free comfort which from thence he hears;
But he bears both the sentence and the sorrow,
That, to pay grief, must of poor patience borrow.
These sentences, to sugar or to gall,
Being strong on both sides, are equivocal:
But words are words; I never yet did hear
That the bruised heart was pierced through the ear.
I humbly beseech you, proceed to the affairs of state.

DUKE. The Turk with a most mighty preparation makes for Cyprus. Othello, the fortitude of the place is best known to you; and though we have there a substitute of most allowed sufficiency, yet opinion, a sovereign mistress of effects, throws a more safer voice on you: you must therefore be content to slubber the gloss of your new fortunes with this more stubborn and boisterous expedition.

OTH. The tyrant custom, most grave senators,
Hath made the flinty and steel couch of war
My thrice-driven bed of down: I do agnize[21]
A natural and prompt alacrity
I find in hardness; and do undertake
These present wars against the Ottomites.
Most humbly therefore bending to your state,
I crave fit disposition for my wife,
Due reference of place and exhibition,
With such accommodation and besort[22]
As levels with her breeding.

DUKE.   If you please,
Be 't at her father's.

BRA.   I 'll not have it so.

OTH. Nor I.

DES.   Nor I, I would not there reside,
To put my father in impatient thoughts
By being in his eye. Most gracious duke,
To my unfolding lend your prosperous ear,
And let me find a charter in your voice
To assist my simpleness.

DUKE. What would you, Desdemona?

DES. That I did love the Moor to live with him,
My downright violence and storm of fortunes
May trumpet to the world: my heart 's subdued

---

21. *agnize*] confess, acknowledge.
22. *besort*] companionship, retinue.

Even to the very quality of my lord:
I saw Othello's visage in his mind,
And to his honours and his valiant parts
Did I my soul and fortunes consecrate.
So that, dear lords, if I be left behind,
A moth[23] of peace, and he go to the war,
The rites for which I love him are bereft me,
And I a heavy interim shall support
By his dear absence. Let me go with him.

OTH.   Let her have your voices.
Vouch with me, heaven, I therefore beg it not,
To please the palate of my appetite;
Nor to comply with heat — the young affects
In me defunct — and proper satisfaction;
But to be free and bounteous to her mind:
And heaven defend your good souls, that you think
I will your serious and great business scant
For she is with me. No, when light-wing'd toys
Of feather'd Cupid seel[24] with wanton dulness
My speculative and officed instruments,[25]
That my disports corrupt and taint my business,
Let housewives make a skillet of my helm,
And all indign[26] and base adversities
Make head against my estimation!

DUKE.   Be it as you shall privately determine,
Either for her stay or going: the affair cries haste,
And speed must answer 't; you must hence to-night.

DES.   To-night, my lord?

DUKE.   This night.

OTH.   With all my heart.

DUKE.   At nine i' the morning here we 'll meet again.
Othello, leave some officer behind,
And he shall our commission bring to you;
With such things else of quality and respect
As doth import you.

OTH.   So please your grace, my ancient;
A man he is of honesty and trust:
To his conveyance I assign my wife,

---

23. A *moth*] An idle parasite.
24. *seel*] close or sew up the eyes.
25. *My . . . instruments*] My faculties of thought or vision and of activity in the discharge
of duty.
26. *indign*] unworthy, disgraceful.

With what else needful your good grace shall think
To be sent after me.

DUKE.   Let it be so.
    Good night to every one. [*To* BRAB.] And, noble signior,
    If virtue no delighted beauty lack,
    Your son-in-law is far more fair than black.

FIRST SEN.   Adieu, brave Moor; use Desdemona well.

BRA.   Look to her, Moor, if thou hast eyes to see:
    She has deceived her father, and may thee.

                        [*Exeunt* Duke, Senators, Officers, &c.]

OTH.   My life upon her faith! Honest Iago,
    My Desdemona must I leave to thee:
    I prithee, let thy wife attend on her;
    And bring them after in the best advantage.
    Come, Desdemona; I have but an hour
    Of love, of worldly matters and direction,
    To spend with thee: we must obey the time.

                        [*Exeunt* OTHELLO *and* DESDEMONA.]

ROD.   Iago!

IAGO.   What say'st thou, noble heart?

ROD.   What will I do, thinkest thou?

IAGO.   Why, go to bed and sleep.

ROD.   I will incontinently drown myself.

IAGO.   If thou dost, I shall never love thee after. Why, thou silly
    gentleman!

ROD.   It is silliness to live when to live is torment; and then have we a
    prescription to die when death is our physician.

IAGO.   O villanous! I have looked upon the world for four times seven
    years; and since I could distinguish betwixt a benefit and an in-
    jury, I never found man that knew how to love himself. Ere I
    would say I would drown myself for the love of a guinea-hen, I
    would change my humanity with a baboon.

ROD.   What should I do? I confess it is my shame to be so fond; but it
    is not in my virtue to amend it.

IAGO.   Virtue! a fig! 't is in ourselves that we are thus or thus. Our
    bodies are gardens; to the which our wills are gardeners: so that
    if we will plant nettles or sow lettuce, set hyssop and weed up
    thyme, supply it with one gender of herbs or distract it with
    many, either to have it sterile with idleness or manured with
    industry, why, the power and corrigible authority of this lies in
    our wills. If the balance of our lives had not one scale of reason
    to poise another of sensuality, the blood and baseness of our na-
    tures would conduct us to most preposterous conclusions: but
    we have reason to cool our raging motions, our carnal stings, our

unbitted lusts; whereof I take this, that you call love, to be a sect
or scion.[27]

ROD. It cannot be.

IAGO. It is merely a lust of the .blood and a permission of the will.
Come, be a man: drown thyself! drown cats and blind puppies.
I have professed me thy friend, and I confess me knit to thy
deserving[28] with cables of perdurable toughness: I could never
better stead thee than now. Put money in thy purse; follow thou
the wars; defeat thy favour[29] with an usurped beard; I say, put
money in thy purse. It cannot be that Desdemona should long
continue her love to the Moor — put money in thy purse — nor
he his to her: it was a violent commencement, and thou shalt
see an answerable sequestration; put but money in thy purse.
These Moors are changeable in their wills: — fill thy purse with
money. The food that to him now is as luscious as locusts, shall
be to him shortly as bitter as coloquintida.[30] She must change
for youth: when she is sated with his body, she will find the error of her choice: she must have change, she must: therefore
put money in thy purse. If thou wilt needs damn thyself, do it
a more delicate way than drowning. Make all the money thou
canst: if sanctimony and a frail vow betwixt an erring barbarian
and a supersubtle Venetian be not too hard for my wits and all the
tribe of hell, thou shalt enjoy her; therefore make money. A pox
of drowning thyself! it is clean out of the way: seek thou rather
to be hanged in compassing thy joy than to be drowned and go
without her.

ROD. Wilt thou be fast to my hopes, if I depend on the issue?

IAGO. Thou art sure of me: go, make money: I have told thee often,
and I re-tell thee again and again, I hate the Moor: my cause is
hearted; thine hath no less reason. Let us be conjunctive in our
revenge against him: if thou canst cuckold him, thou dost thyself
a pleasure, me a sport. There are many events in the womb of
time, which will be delivered. Traverse; go; provide thy money.
We will have more of this to-morrow. Adieu.

ROD. Where shall we meet i' the morning?

IAGO. At my lodging.

ROD. I 'll be with thee betimes.

IAGO. Go to; farewell. Do you hear, Roderigo?

---

27. *a sect or scion*] a cutting or graft.

28. *thy deserving*] thy merits, deserts.

29. *defeat thy favour*] disfigure or disguise your countenance.

30. *coloquintida*] more familiarly known as "colocynth," made from "bitter" apples, a familiar
ingredient in pills.

ROD. What say you?
IAGO. No more of drowning, do you hear?
ROD. I am changed: I 'll go sell all my land.   [*Exit.*]
IAGO. Thus do I ever make my fool my purse;
  For I mine own gain'd knowledge should profane,
  If I would time expend with such a snipe
  But for my sport and profit. I hate the Moor;
  And it is thought abroad that 'twixt my sheets
  He has done my office: I know not if 't be true;
  But I for mere suspicion in that kind
  Will do as if for surety. He holds me well;[31]
  The better shall my purpose work on him.
  Cassio 's a proper[32] man: let me see now;
  To get his place, and to plume up my will
  In double knavery — How, how? — Let 's see: —
  After some time, to abuse Othello's ear
  That he is too familiar with his wife.
  He hath a person and a smooth dispose[33]
  To be suspected; framed to make women false.
  The Moor is of a free and open nature,
  That thinks men honest that but seem to be so;
  And will as tenderly be led by the nose
  As asses are.
  I have 't. It is engender'd. Hell and night
  Must bring this monstrous birth to the world's light. [*Exit.*]

ACT II.

SCENE I. A *Sea-Port in Cyprus. An Open Place Near the Quay.*

Enter MONTANO *and two* Gentlemen

MON. What from the cape can you discern at sea?
FIRST GENT. Nothing at all: it is a high-wrought flood;
  I cannot, 'twixt the heaven and the main,
  Descry a sail.

---

31. *He holds me well*] He thinks well of me.
32. *proper*] handsome.
33. *a smooth dispose*] a smooth or gentle disposition or manner.

MON.   Methinks the wind hath spoke aloud at land;
        A fuller blast ne'er shook our battlements:
        If it hath ruffian'd[1] so upon the sea,
        What ribs of oak, when mountains melt on them,
        Can hold the mortise? What shall we hear of this?
SEC. GENT.   A segregation of the Turkish fleet:
        For do but stand upon the foaming shore,
        The chidden billow seems to pelt the clouds;
        The wind-shaked surge, with high and monstrous mane,
        Seems to cast water on the burning bear,[2]
        And quench the guards of the ever-fixed pole:
        I never did like molestation view
        On the enchafed flood.
MON.   If that the Turkish fleet
        Be not enshelter'd and embay'd, they are drown'd;
        It is impossible to bear it out.

Enter a third Gentleman

THIRD GENT.   News, lads! our wars are done.
        The desperate tempest hath so bang'd the Turks,
        That their designment halts: a noble ship of Venice
        Hath seen a grievous wreck and sufferance
        On most part of their fleet.
MON.   How! is this true?
THIRD GENT.   The ship is here put in,
        A Veronesa; Michael Cassio,
        Lieutenant to the warlike Moor Othello,
        Is come on shore: the Moor himself at sea,
        And is in full commission here for Cyprus.
MON.   I am glad on 't; 't is a worthy governor.
THIRD GENT.   But this same Cassio, though he speak of comfort
        Touching the Turkish loss, yet he looks sadly
        And prays the Moor be safe; for they were parted
        With foul and violent tempest.
MON.   Pray heavens he be;
        For I have served him, and the man commands
        Like a full soldier. Let 's to the seaside, ho!
        As well to see the vessel that 's come in
        As to throw out our eyes for brave Othello,

---

    1. *ruffian'd*] blustered.
    2. *the burning bear*] the shining constellation of the Great Bear, the "ursa major" in the
    northern sky.

      Even till we make the main and the aerial blue
      An indistinct regard.
THIRD GENT.   Come, let 's do so;
      For every minute is expectancy
      Of more arrivance.

Enter CASSIO

CAS.   .Thanks, you the valiant of this warlike isle,
      That so approve the Moor! O, let the heavens
      Give him defence against the elements,
      For I have lost him on a dangerous sea.
MON.   Is he well shipp'd?
CAS.   His bark is stoutly timber'd, and his pilot
      Of very expert and approved allowance;
      Therefore my hopes, not surfeited to death,
      Stand in bold cure.   [*A cry within:* "A sail, a sail, a sail!"]

Enter a fourth Gentleman

CAS.   What noise?
FOURTH GENT.   The town is empty; on the brow o' the sea
      Stand ranks of people, and they cry "A sail!"
CAS.   My hopes do shape him for the governor.   [*Guns heard.*]
SEC. GENT.   They do discharge their shot of courtesy:
      Our friends at least.
CAS.   I pray you, sir, go forth,
      And give us truth who 't is that is arrived.
SEC. GENT.   I shall.   [*Exit.*]

MON.   But, good lieutenant, is your general wived?
CAS.   Most fortunately: he hath achieved a maid
      That paragons description and wild fame;
      One that excels the quirks of blazoning pens,
      And in the essential vesture of creation
      Does tire the ingener.[3]

Re-enter second Gentleman

                    How now! who has put in?
SEC. GENT.   'T is one Iago, ancient to the general.
CAS.   He has had most favourable and happy speed:

---

3. *ingener*] designer, author.

Tempests themselves, high seas, and howling winds,
The gutter'd rocks, and congregated sands,
Traitors ensteep'd to clog the guiltless keel,
As having sense of beauty, do omit
Their mortal natures, letting go safely by
The divine Desdemona.

MON.   What is she?

CAS.   She that I spake of, our great captain's captain,
Left in the conduct of the bold Iago;
Whose footing here anticipates our thoughts
A se'nnight's speed. Great Jove, Othello guard,
And swell his sail with thine own powerful breath,
That he may bless this bay with his tall ship,
Make love's quick pants in Desdemona's arms,
Give renew'd fire to our extinct spirits,
And bring all Cyprus comfort.

Enter DESDEMONA, EMILIA, IAGO, RODERIGO, *and* Attendants

                                   O, behold,
The riches of the ship is come on shore!
Ye men of Cyprus, let her have your knees.
Hail to thee, lady! and the grace of heaven,
Before, behind thee, and on every hand,
Enwheel thee round!

DES.   I thank you, valiant Cassio.
What tidings can you tell me of my lord?

CAS.   He is not yet arrived: nor know I aught
But that he's well and will be shortly here.

DES.   O, but I fear — How lost you company?

CAS.   The great contention of the sea and skies
Parted our fellowship — But, hark! a sail.
                         [*A cry within:* "A sail, a sail!" *Guns heard.*]

SEC. GENT.   They give their greeting to the citadel:
This likewise is a friend.

CAS.   See for the news.   [*Exit* Gentleman.]
Good ancient, you are welcome. [*To* EMILIA] Welcome, mistress:
Let it not gall your patience, good Iago,
That I extend my manners; 't is my breeding
That gives me this bold show of courtesy.   [*Kissing her.*]

IAGO.   Sir, would she give you so much of her lips
As of her tongue she oft bestows on me,
You 'ld have enough.

DES.   Alas, she has no speech.

IAGO.   In faith, too much;
 I find it still when I have list[4] to sleep:
 Marry, before your ladyship, I grant,
 She puts her tongue a little in her heart
 And chides with thinking.
EMIL.   You have little cause to say so.
IAGO.   Come on, come on; you are pictures[5] out of doors,
 Bells in your parlours, wild-cats in your kitchens,
 Saints in your injuries,[6] devils being offended,
 Players in your housewifery, and housewives[7] in your beds.
DES.   O, fie upon thee, slanderer!
IAGO.   Nay, it is true, or else I am a Turk:
 You rise to play, and go to bed to work.
EMIL.   You shall not write my praise.
IAGO.   No, let me not.
DES.   What wouldst thou write of me, if thou shouldst praise me?
IAGO.   O gentle lady, do not put me to 't;
 For I am nothing if not critical.
DES.   Come on, assay — There 's one gone to the harbour?
IAGO.   Ay, madam.
DES.   I am not merry; but I do beguile
 The thing I am by seeming otherwise.
 Come, how wouldst thou praise me?
IAGO.   I am about it; but indeed my invention
 Comes from my pate as birdlime does from frize;[8]
 It plucks out brains and all: but my Muse labours,
 And thus she is deliver'd.
 If she be fair and wise, fairness and wit,
 The one 's for use, the other useth it.
DES.   Well praised! How if she be black and witty?
IAGO.   If she be black, and thereto have a wit,
 She 'll find a white that shall her blackness fit.
DES.   Worse and worse.
EMIL.   How if fair and foolish?
IAGO.   She never yet was foolish that was fair;
 For even her folly help'd her to an heir.

---

4. *have list*] have inclination.
5. *pictures*] beautiful painted objects.
6. *Saints in your injuries*] Assume the meek air of saints when you are bent on injuring others.
7. *housewives*] hussies, with an implication of wantonness.
8. *as birdlime . . . frize*] birdlime was a sticky substance used to trap birds; frize was a coarse woollen material.

DES.   These are old fond[9] paradoxes to make fools laugh i' the ale-
       house. What miserable praise hast thou for her that 's foul and
       foolish?

IAGO.   There's none so foul, and foolish thereunto,
        But does foul pranks which fair and wise ones do.

DES.   O heavy ignorance! thou praisest the worst best. But what praise
       couldst thou bestow on a deserving woman indeed, one that in
       the authority of her merit did justly put on the vouch of very
       malice itself?

IAGO.   She that was ever fair and never proud,
        Had tongue at will and yet was never loud,
        Never lack'd gold and yet went never gay,
        Fled from her wish and yet said "Now I may;"
        She that, being anger'd, her revenge being nigh,
        Bade her wrong stay and her displeasure fly;
        She that in wisdom never was so frail
        To change the cod's head for the salmon's tail;[10]
        She that could think and ne'er disclose her mind,
        See suitors following and not look behind;
        She was a wight, if ever such wight were, —

DES.   To do what?

IAGO.   To suckle fools and chronicle small beer.[11]

DES.   O most lame and impotent conclusion! Do not learn of him,
       Emilia, though he be thy husband. How say you, Cassio? is he
       not a most profane and liberal counsellor?

CAS.   He speaks home,[12] madam: you may relish him more in the
       soldier than in the scholar.

IAGO.   [Aside] He takes her by the palm: ay, well said, whisper: with as
        little a web as this will I ensnare as great a fly as Cassio. Ay, smile
        upon her, do; I will gyve thee in thine own courtship. You say
        true; 't is so, indeed: if such tricks as these strip you out of your
        lieutenantry, it had been better you had not kissed your three fin-
        gers so oft, which now again you are most apt to play the sir in.
        Very good; well kissed! an excellent courtesy! 't is so, indeed. Yet
        again your fingers to your lips? would they were clyster-pipes for
        your sake! — [Trumpet within.] The Moor! I know his trumpet.

CAS.   'T is truly so.

DES.   Let 's meet him and receive him.

CAS.   Lo, where he comes!

---

9. *fond*] silly.

10. *change . . . tail*] give up a delicacy (cod's head) in exchange for coarse fare (salmon's tail).

11. *chronicle small beer*] keep account of small household expenses.

12. *home*] to the quick, so as to make the intended effect.

Enter OTHELLO *and* Attendants

OTH.　O my fair warrior!
DES.　　　　　　　My dear Othello!
OTH.　It gives me wonder great as my content
　　　To see you here before me. O my soul's joy!
　　　If after every tempest come such calms,
　　　May the winds blow till they have waken'd death!
　　　And let the labouring bark climb hills of seas
　　　Olympus-high, and duck again as low
　　　As hell's from heaven! If it were now to die,
　　　'T were now to be most happy; for I fear,
　　　My soul hath her content so absolute
　　　That not another comfort like to this
　　　Succeeds in unknown fate.
DES.　　　　　　　The heavens forbid
　　　But that our loves and comforts should increase,
　　　Even as our days do grow!
OTH.　　　　　　Amen to that, sweet powers!
　　　I cannot speak enough of this content;
　　　It stops me here; it is too much of joy:
　　　And this, and this, the greatest discords be　　　[*Kissing her.*]
　　　That e'er our hearts shall make!
IAGO.　　　　　[*Aside*]　O, you are well tuned now!
　　　But I'll set down the pegs that make this music,
　　　As honest as I am.
OTH.　　　　　Come, let us to the castle.
　　　News, friends; our wars are done, the Turks are drown'd.
　　　How does my old acquaintance of this isle?
　　　Honey, you shall be well desired in Cyprus;
　　　I have found great love amongst them. O my sweet,
　　　I prattle out of fashion, and I dote
　　　In mine own comforts. I prithee, good Iago,
　　　Go to the bay, and disembark my coffers:
　　　Bring thou the master to the citadel;
　　　He is a good one, and his worthiness
　　　Does challenge much respect. Come, Desdemona,
　　　Once more well met at Cyprus.
　　　　　　　　　[*Exeunt all but* IAGO *and* RODERIGO.]
IAGO.　Do thou meet me presently at the harbour. Come hither. If thou
　　　be'st valiant — as, they say, base men being in love have then a
　　　nobility in their natures more than is native to them — list me.
　　　The lieutenant to-night watches on the court of guard. First, I
　　　must tell thee this: Desdemona is directly in love with him.

ROD.   With him! why, 't is not possible.

IAGO.   Lay thy finger thus,[13] and let thy soul be instructed. Mark me with what violence she first loved the Moor, but for bragging and telling her fantastical lies: and will she love him still for prating? let not thy discreet heart think it. Her eye must be fed; and what delight shall she have to look on the devil? When the blood is made dull with the act of sport, there should be, again to inflame it and to give satiety a fresh appetite, loveliness in favour, sympathy in years, manners and beauties; all which the Moor is defective in: now, for want of these required conveniences, her delicate tenderness will find itself abused, begin to heave the gorge, disrelish and abhor the Moor; very nature will instruct her in it and compel her to some second choice. Now, sir, this granted — as it is a most pregnant and unforced position — who stands so eminently in the degree of this fortune as Cassio does? a knave very voluble; no further conscionable than in putting on the mere form of civil and humane seeming, for the better compassing of his salt and most hidden loose affection? why, none; why, none: a slipper[14] and subtle knave; a finder out of occasions; that has an eye can stamp and counterfeit advantages, though true advantage never present itself: a devilish knave! Besides, the knave is handsome, young, and hath all those requisites in him that folly and green minds look after: a pestilent complete knave; and the woman hath found him already.

ROD.   I cannot believe that in her; she 's full of most blest condition.

IAGO.   Blest fig's-end! the wine she drinks is made of grapes: if she had been blest, she would never have loved the Moor: blest pudding! Didst thou not see her paddle with the palm of his hand? didst not mark that?

ROD.   Yes, that I did; but that was but courtesy.

IAGO.   Lechery, by this hand; an index and obscure prologue to the history of lust and foul thoughts. They met so near with their lips that their breaths embraced together. Villanous thoughts, Roderigo! when these mutualities so marshal the way, hard at hand comes the master and main exercise, the incorporate conclusion: pish! But, sir, be you ruled by me: I have brought you from Venice. Watch you to-night; for the command, I 'll lay 't upon you: Cassio knows you not: I 'll not be far from you: do you find some occasion to anger Cassio, either by speaking too loud, or tainting his discipline, or from what other course you please, which the time shall more favourably minister.

---

13. *Lay thy finger thus*] Iago puts his finger to his lips, enjoining silence on Roderigo.
14. *slipper*] an old form of "slippery."

ROD.   Well.

IAGO.   Sir, he is rash and very sudden in choler, and haply may strike at
you: provoke him, that he may; for even out of that will I cause
these of Cyprus to mutiny; whose qualification shall come into
no true taste again but by the displanting of Cassio. So shall
you have a shorter journey to your desires by the means I shall
then have to prefer them, and the impediment most profitably
removed, without the which there were no expectation of our
prosperity.

ROD.   I will do this, if I can bring it to any opportunity.

IAGO.   I warrant thee. Meet me by and by at the citadel: I must fetch
his necessaries ashore. Farewell.

                                                  [*Exit.*]

ROD.   Adieu.

IAGO.   That Cassio loves her, I do well believe it;
That she loves him, 't is apt and of great credit:[15]
The Moor, howbeit that I endure him not,
Is of a constant, loving, noble nature;
And I dare think he 'll prove to Desdemona
A most dear husband. Now, I do love her too,
Not out of absolute lust, though peradventure
I stand accountant for as great a sin,
But partly led to diet my revenge,
For that I do suspect the lusty Moor
Hath leap'd into my seat: the thought whereof
Doth like a poisonous mineral gnaw my inwards;
And nothing can or shall content my soul
Till I am even'd with him, wife for wife;
Or failing so, yet that I put the Moor
At least into a jealousy so strong
That judgement cannot cure. Which thing to do,
If this poor trash of Venice, whom I trash[16]
For his quick hunting, stand the putting on,
I 'll have our Michael Cassio on the hip,
Abuse him to the Moor in the rank garb;
For I fear Cassio with my night-cap too;
Make the Moor thank me, love me and reward me,
For making him egregiously an ass
And practising upon his peace and quiet
Even to madness. 'T is here,[17] but yet confused:
Knavery's plain face is never seen till used.

                                                  [*Exit.*]

---

15. *apt . . . credit*] natural and most credible.
16. *trash . . . trash*] the noun "trash" here means worthless people; the verb "trash" is a hunting
term, meaning to restrain with a leash.
17. *'T is here*] Iago raises his hand to his head.

SCENE II. A *Street*.

Enter a Herald *with a proclamation; People following*

HER.   It is Othello's pleasure, our noble and valiant general, that upon
certain tidings now arrived, importing the mere perdition of
the Turkish fleet, every man put himself into triumph; some to
dance, some to make bonfires, each man to what sport and revels
his addiction leads him: for, besides these beneficial news, it is
the celebration of his nuptial. So much was his pleasure should
be proclaimed. All offices[1] are open, and there is full liberty
of feasting from this present hour of five till the bell have told
eleven. Heaven bless the isle of Cyprus and our noble general
Othello!   [*Exeunt.*]

SCENE III. A *Hall in the Castle*.

Enter OTHELLO, DESDEMONA, CASSIO, *and* Attendants

OTH.   Good Michael, look you to the guard to-night:
    Let 's teach ourselves that honourable stop,
    Not to outsport discretion.
CAS.   Iago hath direction what to do;
    But notwithstanding with my personal eye
    Will I look to 't.
OTH.   Iago is most honest.
    Michael, good night: to-morrow with your earliest
    Let me have speech with you. Come, my dear love,
    The purchase made, the fruits are to ensue;
    That profit 's yet to come 'tween me and you.
    Good night.   [*Exeunt* OTHELLO, DESDEMONA, *and* Attendants.]

Enter IAGO

CAS.   Welcome, Iago; we must to the watch.
IAGO.   Not this hour, lieutenant; 't is not yet ten o' the clock. Our gen-
    eral cast us thus early for the love of his Desdemona; who let us

---

1. *offices*] rooms in the castle where stores of food and drink were kept.

not therefore blame: he hath not yet made wanton the night with
her, and she is sport for Jove.

CAS. She 's a most exquisite lady.

IAGO. And, I 'll warrant her, full of game.

CAS. Indeed she 's a most fresh and delicate creature.

IAGO. What an eye she has! methinks it sounds a parley to provocation.

CAS. An inviting eye; and yet methinks right modest.

IAGO. And when she speaks, is it not an alarum to love?

CAS. She is indeed perfection.

IAGO. Well, happiness to their sheets! Come, lieutenant, I have a
stoup[1] of wine; and here without are a brace of Cyprus gallants that would fain have a measure to the health of black
Othello.

CAS. Not to-night, good Iago: I have very poor and unhappy brains for
drinking: I could well wish courtesy would invent some other
custom of entertainment.

IAGO. O, they are our friends; but one cup: I 'll drink for you.

CAS. I have drunk but one cup to-night, and that was craftily quali-
fied too, and behold what innovation it makes here: I am unfortunate in the infirmity, and dare not task my weakness with any
more.

IAGO. What, man! 't is a night of revels: the gallants desire it.

CAS. Where are they?

IAGO. Here at the door; I pray you, call them in.

CAS. I 'll do 't; but it dislikes me.   [*Exit.*]

IAGO. If I can fasten but one cup upon him,
With that which he hath drunk to-night already,
He 'll be as full of quarrel and offence
As my young mistress' dog. Now my sick fool Roderigo,
Whom love hath turn'd almost the wrong side out,
To Desdemona hath to-night caroused
Potations pottle-deep;[2] and he 's to watch:
Three lads of Cyprus, noble swelling spirits,
That hold their honours in a wary distance,
The very elements of this warlike isle,
Have I to-night fluster'd with flowing cups,
And they watch too. Now, 'mongst this flock of drunkards,
Am I to put our Cassio in some action
That may offend the isle. But here they come:
If consequence do but approve my dream,

---

1. *a stoup*] a large tankard.
2. *pottle-deep*] a "pottle" was a measure of two quarts.

My boat sails freely, both with wind and stream.

Re-enter CASSIO; *with him* MONTANO *and* Gentlemen; *Servants follow-ing with wine*

CAS.   'Fore God, they have given me a rouse[3] already.
MON.   Good faith, a little one; not past a pint, as I am a soldier.
IAGO.   Some wine, ho!

> [*Sings*]   And let me the canakin clink, clink;
> And let me the canakin clink:
> A soldier 's a man;
> A life 's but a span;
> Why then let a soldier drink.

Some wine, boys!
CAS.   'Fore God, an excellent song.
IAGO.   I learned it in England, where indeed they are most potent
in potting: your Dane, your German, and your swag-bellied
Hollander, — Drink, ho! — are nothing to your English.
CAS.   Is your Englishman so expert in his drinking?
IAGO.   Why, he drinks you with facility your Dane dead drunk; he
sweats not to overthrow your Almain; he gives your Hollander a
vomit ere the next pottle can be filled.
CAS.   To the health of our general!
MON.   I am for it, lieutenant, and I 'll do you justice.
IAGO.   O sweet England!

> [*Sings*]   King Stephen was a worthy peer,
> His breeches cost him but a crown;
> He held them sixpence all too dear,
> With that he call'd the tailor lown.
>
> He was a wight of high renown,
> And thou art but of low degree:
> 'T is pride that pulls the country down;
> Then take thine auld cloak about thee.

Some wine, ho!
CAS.   Why, this is a more exquisite song than the other.
IAGO.   Will you hear 't again?
CAS.   No; for I hold him to be unworthy of his place that does those
things. Well: God 's above all; and there be souls must be saved,
and there be souls must not be saved.

---

3. *a rouse*] a full measure of liquor.

IAGO.   It 's true, good lieutenant.

CAS.   For mine own part — no offence to the general, nor any man of
quality — I hope to be saved.

IAGO.   And so do I too, lieutenant.

CAS.   Ay, but, by your leave, not before me; the lieutenant is to be saved
before the ancient. Let 's have no more of this; let 's to our affairs.
God forgive us our sins! Gentlemen, let 's look to our business.
Do not think, gentlemen, I am drunk: this is my ancient: this is
my right hand, and this is my left. I am not drunk now; I can
stand well enough, and speak well enough.

ALL.   Excellent well.

CAS.   Why, very well then; you must not think then that I am
drunk.   [*Exit.*]

MON.   To the platform, masters; come, let 's set the watch.

IAGO.   You see this fellow that is gone before;
He is a soldier fit to stand by Cæsar
And give direction: and do but see his vice;
'T is to his virtue a just equinox,
The one as long as the other: 't is pity of him.
I fear the trust Othello puts him in
On some odd time of his infirmity
Will shake this island.

MON.   But is he often thus?

IAGO.   'T is evermore the prologue to his sleep:
He 'll watch the horologe[4] a double set,
If drink rock not his cradle.

MON.   It were well
The general were put in mind of it.
Perhaps he sees it not, or his good nature
Prizes the virtue that appears in Cassio
And looks not on his evils: is not this true?

Enter RODERIGO

IAGO.   [*Aside to him*] How now, Roderigo!
I pray you, after the lieutenant; go.   [*Exit* RODERIGO.]

MON.   And 't is great pity that the noble Moor
Should hazard such a place as his own second
With one of an ingraft[5] infirmity:
It were an honest action to say
So to the Moor.

---

4. *horologe*] clock.
5. *ingraft*] inveterate, rooted.

IAGO.   Not I, for this fair island:
   I do love Cassio well, and would do much
   To cure him of this evil: — But, hark! what noise?
                [A *cry within:* "Help! help!"]

Re-enter CASSIO, *driving in* RODERIGO

CAS.   'Zounds! you rogue! you rascal!
MON.   What's the matter, lieutenant?
CAS.   A knave teach me my duty! But I 'll beat the knave into a wicker
   bottle.
ROD.   Beat me!
CAS.   Dost thou prate, rogue?   [*Striking* RODERIGO.]
MON.   Nay, good lieutenant; I pray you, sir, hold your hand.
CAS.   Let me go, sir, or I 'll knock you o'er the mazzard.[6]
MON.   Come, come, you 're drunk.
CAS.   Drunk!   [*They fight.*]
IAGO.   [*Aside to* RODERIGO] Away, I say; go out, and cry a mutiny.
                       [*Exit* RODERIGO.]
   Nay, good lieutenant! God's will, gentlemen!
   Help, ho! — Lieutenant, — sir, — Montano, — sir; —
   Help, masters! — Here 's a goodly watch indeed!   [A *bell rings.*]
   Who 's that that rings the bell? — Diablo, ho!
   The town will rise: God's will, lieutenant, hold;
   You will be shamed for ever.

Re-enter OTHELLO *and* Attendants

OTH.   What is the matter here?
MON.   'Zounds, I bleed still; I am hurt to the death.   [*Faints.*]
OTH.   Hold, for your lives!
IAGO.   Hold, ho! Lieutenant, — sir, — Montano, — gentlemen, —
   Have you forgot all sense of place and duty?
   Hold! the general speaks to you; hold, hold, for shame!
OTH.   Why, how now, ho! from whence ariseth this?
   Are we turn'd Turks, and to ourselves do that
   Which heaven hath forbid the Ottomites?
   For Christian shame, put by this barbarous brawl:
   He that stirs next to carve for his own rage
   Holds his soul light; he dies upon his motion.
   Silence that dreadful bell: it frights the isle
   From her propriety. What is the matter, masters?

---

6. *mazzard*] head.

   Honest Iago, that look'st dead with grieving,
   Speak, who began this? on thy love, I charge thee.
IAGO. I do not know: friends all but now, even now,
   In quarter, and in terms like bride and groom
   Devesting them for bed; and then, but now,
   As if some planet had unwitted men,
   Swords out, and tilting one at other's breast,
   In opposition bloody. I cannot speak
   Any beginning to this peevish odds;
   And would in action glorious I had lost
   Those legs that brought me to a part of it!
OTH. How comes it, Michael, you are thus forgot?
CAS. I pray you, pardon me; I cannot speak.
OTH. Worthy Montano, you were wont be civil;
   The gravity and stillness of your youth
   The world hath noted, and your name is great
   In mouths of wisest censure: what 's the matter,
   That you unlace your reputation thus,
   And spend your rich opinion for the name
   Of a night-brawler? give me answer to it.
MON. Worthy Othello, I am hurt to danger:
   Your officer, Iago, can inform you —
   While I spare speech, which something now offends me —
   Of all that I do know: nor know I aught
   By me that 's said or done amiss this night;
   Unless self-charity be sometimes a vice,
   And to defend ourselves it be a sin
   When violence assails us.
OTH.   Now, by heaven,
   My blood begins my safer guides to rule,
   And passion, having my best judgement collied,[7]
   Assays to lead the way: if I once stir,
   Or do but lift this arm, the best of you
   Shall sink in my rebuke. Give me to know
   How this foul rout began, who set it on,
   And he that is approved in this offence,
   Though he had twinn'd with me, both at a birth,
   Shall lose me. What! in a town of war,
   Yet wild, the people's hearts brimful of fear,
   To manage private and domestic quarrel,
   In night, and on the court and guard of safety!
   'T is monstrous. Iago, who began 't?

---

7. *collied*] blackened, darkened.

MON.   If partially affined,[8] or leagued in office,
    Thou dost deliver more or less than truth,
    Thou art no soldier.
IAGO.   Touch me not so near:
    I had rather have this tongue cut from my mouth
    Than it should do offence to Michael Cassio;
    Yet, I persuade myself, to speak the truth
    Shall nothing wrong him. Thus it is, general.
    Montano and myself being in speech,
    There comes a fellow crying out for help,
    And Cassio following him with determined sword,
    To execute upon him. Sir, this gentleman
    Steps in to Cassio and entreats his pause:
    Myself the crying fellow did pursue,
    Lest by his clamour — as it so fell out —
    The town might fall in fright: he, swift of foot,
    Outran my purpose; and I return'd the rather
    For that I heard the clink and fall of swords,
    And Cassio high in oath; which till to-night
    I ne'er might say before. When I came back —
    For this was brief — I found them close together,
    At blow and thrust; even as again they were
    When you yourself did part them.
    More of this matter cannot I report:
    But men are men; the best sometimes forget:
    Though Cassio did some little wrong to him,
    As men in rage strike those that wish them best,
    Yet surely Cassio, I believe, received
    From him that fled some strange indignity,
    Which patience could not pass.
OTH.   I know, Iago,
    Thy honesty and love doth mince this matter,
    Making it light to Cassio. Cassio, I love thee;
    But never more be officer of mine.

Re-enter DESDEMONA, *attended*

    Look, if my gentle love be not raised up!
    I 'll make thee an example.
DES.   What 's the matter?
OTH.   All 's well now, sweeting; come away to bed.

---

    8. *partially affined*] connected by close ties, which would result in a partial account of
the fight.

Sir, for your hurts, myself will be your surgeon:
> [*To* MONTANO, *who is led off.*]

Lead him off.
Iago, look with care about the town,
And silence those whom this vile brawl distracted.
Come, Desdemona: 't is the soldiers' life
To have their balmy slumbers waked with strife.
> [*Exeunt all but* IAGO *and* CASSIO.]

IAGO. What, are you hurt, lieutenant?

CAS. Ay, past all surgery.

IAGO. Marry, heaven forbid!

CAS. Reputation, reputation, reputation! O, I have lost my reputation! I have lost the immortal part of myself, and what remains is bestial. My reputation, Iago, my reputation!

IAGO. As I am an honest man, I thought you had received some bodily wound; there is more sense in that than in reputation. Reputation is an idle and most false imposition; oft got without merit and lost without deserving: you have lost no reputation at all, unless you repute yourself such a loser. What, man! there are ways to recover the general again: you are but now cast in his mood, a punishment more in policy than in malice; even so as one would beat his offenceless dog to affright an imperious lion: sue to him again, and he 's yours.

CAS. I will rather sue to be despised than to deceive so good a commander with so slight, so drunken, and so indiscreet an officer. Drunk? and speak parrot?[9] and squabble? swagger? swear? and discourse fustian[10] with one's own shadow? O thou invisible spirit of wine, if thou hast no name to be known by, let us call thee devil!

IAGO. What was he that you followed with your sword? What had he done to you?

CAS. I know not.

IAGO. Is 't possible?

CAS. I remember a mass of things, but nothing distinctly; a quarrel, but nothing wherefore. O God, that men should put an enemy in their mouths to steal away their brains! that we should, with joy, pleasance, revel and applause, transform ourselves into beasts!

IAGO. Why, but you are now well enough: how came you thus recovered?

CAS. It hath pleased the devil drunkenness to give place to the devil

---

9. *speak parrot?*] speak as senselessly as a parrot.
10. *fustian*] high-sounding nonsense.

wrath: one unperfectness shows me another, to make me frankly despise myself.

IAGO.   Come, you are too severe a moraler: as the time, the place, and the condition of this country stands, I could heartily wish this had not befallen; but since it is as it is, mend it for your own good.

CAS.   I will ask him for my place again; he shall tell me I am a drunkard! Had I as many mouths as Hydra, such an answer would stop them all. To be now a sensible man, by and by a fool, and presently a beast! O strange! Every inordinate cup is unblest, and the ingredient is a devil.

IAGO.   Come, come, good wine is a good familiar creature, if it be well used: exclaim no more against it. And, good lieutenant, I think you think I love you.

CAS.   I have well approved it, sir. I drunk!

IAGO.   You or any man living may be drunk at some time, man. I 'll tell you what you shall do. Our general's wife is now the general. I may say so in this respect, for that he hath devoted and given up himself to the contemplation, mark and denotement of her parts and graces: confess yourself freely to her; importune her help to put you in your place again: she is of so free, so kind, so apt, so blessed a disposition, she holds it a vice in her goodness not to do more than she is requested: this broken joint between you and her husband entreat her to splinter; and, my fortunes against any lay worth naming, this crack of your love shall grow stronger than it was before.

CAS.   You advise me well.

IAGO.   I protest, in the sincerity of love and honest kindness.

CAS.   I think it freely; and betimes in the morning I will beseech the virtuous Desdemona to undertake for me: I am desperate of my fortunes if they check me here.

IAGO.   You are in the right. Good night, lieutenant; I must to the watch.

CAS.   Good night, honest Iago.   [*Exit.*]

IAGO.   And what 's he then that says I play the villain?
When this advice is free I give and honest,
Probal[11] to thinking, and indeed the course
To win the Moor again? For 't is most easy
The inclining Desdemona to subdue
In any honest suit. She 's framed as fruitful[12]
As the free elements. And then for her
To win the Moor, were 't to renounce his baptism,
All seals and symbols of redeemed sin,

---

11. *Probal*] Contraction of "probable."
12. *fruitful*] bountiful, benign.

His soul is so enfetter'd to her love,
That she may make, unmake, do what she list,
Even as her appetite shall play the god
With his weak function. How am I then a villain
To counsel Cassio to this parallel course,
Directly to his good? Divinity of hell!
When devils will the blackest sins put on,
They do suggest at first with heavenly shows,
As I do now: for whiles this honest fool
Plies Desdemona to repair his fortunes,
And she for him pleads strongly to the Moor,
I 'll pour this pestilence into his ear,
That she repeals him for her body's lust;
And by how much she strives to do him good,
She shall undo her credit with the Moor.
So will I turn her virtue into pitch;
And out of her own goodness make the net
That shall enmesh them all.

Enter RODERIGO

                              How now, Roderigo!
ROD.   I do follow here in the chase, not like a hound that hunts, but one
       that fills up the cry.[13] My money is almost spent; I have been to-
       night exceedingly well cudgelled; and I think the issue will be,
       I shall have so much experience for my pains; and so, with no
       money at all and a little more wit, return again to Venice.
IAGO.   How poor are they that have not patience!
       What wound did ever heal but by degrees?
       Thou know'st we work by wit and not by witchcraft,
       And wit depends on dilatory time.
       Does 't not go well? Cassio hath beaten thee,
       And thou by that small hurt hast cashier'd Cassio:
       Though other things grow fair against the sun,
       Yet fruits that blossom first will first be ripe:
       Content thyself awhile. By the mass, 't is morning;
       Pleasure and action make the hours seem short.
       Retire thee; go where thou art billeted:
       Away, I say; thou shalt know more hereafter:
       Nay, get thee gone. [*Exit* ROD.] Two things are to be done:
       My wife must move for Cassio to her mistress;
       I 'll set her on;

---

13. *the cry*] a common term for a pack of hounds.

Myself the while to draw the Moor apart,
And bring him jump[14] when he may Cassio find
Soliciting his wife: ay, that 's the way;
Dull not device by coldness and delay.   [*Exit.*]

ACT III.

SCENE I. *Before the Castle.*

Enter CASSIO *and some* Musicians

CAS.   Masters, play here; I will content your pains;
    Something that 's brief; and bid "Good morrow, general."

                                                          [*Music.*]

Enter Clown

CLO.   Why, masters, have your instruments been in Naples, that they
    speak i' the nose thus?
FIRST MUS.   How, sir, how?
CLO.   Are these, I pray you, wind-instruments?
FIRST MUS.   Ay, marry, are they, sir.
CLO.   O, thereby hangs a tail.
FIRST MUS.   Whereby hangs a tale, sir?
CLO.   Marry, sir, by many a wind-instrument that I know. But, masters,
    here 's money for you: and the general so likes your music, that
    he desires you, for love's sake, to make no more noise with it.
FIRST MUS.   Well, sir, we will not.
CLO.   If you have any music that may not be heard, to 't again: but, as
    they say, to hear music the general does not greatly care.
FIRST MUS.   We have none such, sir.
CLO.   Then put up your pipes in your bag, for I 'll away: go; vanish into
    air; away!   [*Exeunt* Musicians.]
CAS.   Dost thou hear, my honest friend?
CLO.   No, I hear not your honest friend; I hear you.
CAS.   Prithee, keep up thy quillets.[1] There's a poor piece of gold for
    thee: if the gentlewoman that attends the general's wife be stir-
    ring, tell her there 's one Cassio entreats her a little favour of
    speech: wilt thou do this?

---

14. *jump*] just, at the very instant.
 1. *quillets*] niceties, verbal distinctions.

CLO. She is stirring, sir: if she will stir hither, I shall seem to notify
unto her.

CAS. Do, good my friend. [*Exit* Clown.]

Enter IAGO

In happy time, Iago.

IAGO. You have not been a-bed, then?

CAS. Why, no; the day had broke
Before we parted. I have made bold, Iago,
To send in to your wife: my suit to her
Is, that she will to virtuous Desdemona
Procure me some access.

IAGO. I 'll send her to you presently;
And I 'll devise a mean to draw the Moor
Out of the way, that your converse and business
May be more free.

CAS. I humbly thank you for 't. [*Exit* IAGO.] I never knew
A Florentine more kind and honest.

Enter EMILIA

EMIL. Good morrow, good lieutenant: I am sorry
For your displeasure; but all will sure be well.
The general and his wife are talking of it,
And she speaks for you stoutly: the Moor replies,
That he you hurt is of great fame in Cyprus
And great affinity, and that in wholesome wisdom
He might not but refuse you; but he protests he loves you,
And needs no other suitor but his likings
To take the safest occasion by the front
To bring you in again.

CAS. Yet, I beseech you,
If you think fit, or that it may be done,
Give me advantage of some brief discourse
With Desdemona alone.

EMIL. Pray you, come in:
I will bestow you where you shall have time
To speak your bosom freely.

CAS. I am much bound to you. [*Exeunt.*]

SCENE II. *A Room in the Castle.*

Enter OTHELLO, IAGO, *and* Gentlemen

OTH.   These letters give, Iago, to the pilot;
     And by him do my duties to the senate:
     That done, I will be walking on the works;
     Repair there to me.
IAGO.   Well, my good lord, I 'll do 't.
OTH.   This fortification, gentlemen, shall we see 't?
GENT.   We 'll wait upon your lordship.   [*Exeunt.*]

SCENE III. *The Garden of the Castle.*

Enter DESDEMONA, CASSIO, *and* EMILIA

DES.   Be thou assured, good Cassio, I will do
     All my abilities in thy behalf.
EMIL.   Good madam, do: I warrant it grieves my husband
     As if the case were his.
DES.   O, that 's an honest fellow. Do not doubt, Cassio,
     But I will have my lord and you again
     As friendly as you were.
CAS.   Bounteous madam,
     Whatever shall become of Michael Cassio,
     He 's never any thing but your true servant.
DES.   I know 't: I thank you. You do love my lord:
     You have known him long; and be you well assured
     He shall in strangeness stand no farther off
     Than in a politic distance.
CAS.   Ay, but, lady,
     That policy may either last so long,
     Or feed upon such nice and waterish diet,
     Or breed itself so out of circumstance,
     That, I being absent and my place supplied,
     My general will forget my love and service.
DES.   Do not doubt[1] that; before Emilia here
     I give thee warrant of thy place: assure thee,
     If I do vow a friendship, I 'll perform it

---

1. *doubt*] fear.

To the last article: my lord shall never rest;
I 'll watch him tame[2] and talk him out of patience;
His bed shall seem a school, his board a shrift;
I 'll intermingle every thing he does
With Cassio's suit: therefore be merry, Cassio;
For thy solicitor shall rather die
Than give thy cause away.

Enter OTHELLO *and* IAGO, *at a distance*

EMIL.   Madam, here comes my lord.
CAS.   Madam, I 'll take my leave.
DES.   Nay, stay and hear me speak.
CAS.   Madam, not now: I am very ill at ease,
    Unfit for mine own purposes.
DES.   Well, do your discretion.   [*Exit* CASSIO.]
IAGO.   Ha! I like not that.
OTH.   What dost thou say?
IAGO.   Nothing, my lord: or if — I know not what.
OTH.   Was not that Cassio parted from my wife?
IAGO.   Cassio, my lord! No, sure, I cannot think it,
    That he would steal away so guilty-like,
    Seeing you coming.
OTH.   I do believe 't was he.
DES.   How now, my lord!
    I have been talking with a suitor here,
    A man that languishes in your displeasure.
OTH.   Who is 't you mean?
DES.   Why, your lieutenant, Cassio. Good my lord,
    If I have any grace or power to move you,
    His present reconciliation take;
    For if he be not one that truly loves you,
    That errs in ignorance and not in cunning,
    I have no judgement in an honest face:
    I prithee, call him back.
OTH.   Went he hence now?
DES.   Ay, sooth; so humbled,
    That he hath left part of his grief with me,
    To suffer with him. Good love, call him back.
OTH.   Not now, sweet Desdemona; some other time.
DES.   But shall 't be shortly?
OTH.   The sooner, sweet, for you.

---

2. *I 'll watch him tame*] Falconers kept hawks awake in order to tame them and make them
obedient.

DES.   Shall 't be to-night at supper?
OTH.   No, not to-night.
DES.   To-morrow dinner then?
OTH.   I shall not dine at home;
    I meet the captains at the citadel.
DES.   Why then to-morrow night; or Tuesday morn;
    On Tuesday noon, or night; on Wednesday morn:
    I prithee, name the time; but let it not
    Exceed three days: in faith, he 's penitent;
    And yet his trespass, in our common reason —
    Save that, they say, the wars must make examples
    Out of their best — is not almost a fault
    To incur a private check. When shall he come?
    Tell me, Othello: I wonder in my soul,
    What you would ask me, that I should deny,
    Or stand so mammering[3] on. What! Michael Cassio,
    That came a-wooing with you, and so many a time
    When I have spoke of you dispraisingly
    Hath ta'en your part; to have so much to do
    To bring him in! Trust me, I could do much —
OTH.   Prithee, no more: let him come when he will;
    I will deny thee nothing.
DES.   Why, this is not a boon;
    'T is as I should entreat you wear your gloves,
    Or feed on nourishing dishes, or keep you warm,
    Or sue to you to do a peculiar profit
    To your own person: nay, when I have a suit
    Wherein I mean to touch[4] your love indeed,
    It shall be full of poise and difficult weight,
    And fearful to be granted.
OTH.   I will deny thee nothing:
    Whereon, I do beseech thee, grant me this,
    To leave me but a little to myself.
DES.   Shall I deny you? no: farewell, my lord.
OTH.   Farewell, my Desdemona: I 'll come to thee straight.
DES.   Emilia, come. Be as your fancies teach you;
    Whate'er you be, I am obedient.

                [*Exeunt* DESDEMONA *and* EMILIA.]
OTH.   Excellent wretch! Perdition catch my soul,
    But I do love thee! and when I love thee not,
    Chaos is come again.

---

3. *mammering*] muttering hesitatingly.
4. *touch*] test, apply the touchstone to.

IAGO.   My noble lord, —

OTH.   What dost thou say, Iago?

IAGO.   Did Michael Cassio, when you woo'd my lady,
     Know of your love?

OTH.   He did, from first to last: why dost thou ask?

IAGO.   But for a satisfaction of my thought;
     No further harm.

OTH.   Why of thy thought, Iago?

IAGO.   I did not think he had been acquainted with her.

OTH.   O, yes, and went between us very oft.

IAGO.   Indeed!

OTH.   Indeed! ay, indeed: discern'st thou aught in that?
     Is he not honest?

IAGO.   Honest, my lord!

OTH.   Honest! ay, honest.

IAGO.   My lord, for aught I know.

OTH.   What dost thou think?

IAGO.   Think, my lord!

OTH.   Think, my lord! By heaven, he echoes me,
     As if there were some monster in his thought
     Too hideous to be shown. Thou dost mean something:
     I heard thee say even now, thou likedst not that,
     When Cassio left my wife: what didst not like?
     And when I told thee he was of my counsel
     In my whole course of wooing, thou criedst "Indeed!"
     And didst contract and purse thy brow together,
     As if thou then hadst shut up in thy brain
     Some horrible conceit: if thou dost love me,
     Show me thy thought.

IAGO.   My lord, you know I love you.

OTH.   I think thou dost;
     And for I know thou 'rt full of love and honesty
     And weigh'st thy words before thou givest them breath,
     Therefore these stops of thine fright me the more:
     For such things in a false disloyal knave
     Are tricks of custom; but in a man that 's just
     They 're close delations,[5] working from the heart,
     That passion cannot rule.

IAGO.   For Michael Cassio,
     I dare be sworn I think that he is honest.

OTH.   I think so too.

IAGO.   Men should be what they seem;

---

5. *delations*] denunciations, accusations.

Or those that be not, would they might seem none!

OTH.   Certain, men should be what they seem.

IAGO.   Why then I think Cassio 's an honest man.

OTH.   Nay, yet there 's more in this:
I prithee, speak to me as to thy thinkings,
As thou dost ruminate, and give thy worst of thoughts
The worst of words.

IAGO.   Good my lord, pardon me:
Though I am bound to every act of duty,
I am not bound to that all slaves are free to.
Utter my thoughts? Why, say they are vile and false;
As where 's that palace whereinto foul things
Sometimes intrude not? who has a breast so pure,
But some uncleanly apprehensions
Keep leets[6] and law-days, and in session sit
With meditations lawful?

OTH.   Thou dost conspire against thy friend, Iago,
If thou but think'st him wrong'd and makest his ear
A stranger to thy thoughts.

IAGO.   I do beseech you —
Though I perchance am vicious in my guess,
As, I confess, it is my nature's plague
To spy into abuses, and oft my jealousy
Shapes faults that are not — that your wisdom yet,
From one that so imperfectly conceits,
Would take no notice, nor build yourself a trouble
Out of his scattering[7] and unsure observance.
It were not for your quiet nor your good,
Nor for my manhood, honesty, or wisdom,
To let you know my thoughts.

OTH.   What dost thou mean?

IAGO.   Good name in man and woman, dear my lord,
Is the immediate jewel of their souls:
Who steals my purse steals trash; 't is something, nothing;
'T was mine, 't is his, and has been slave to thousands;
But he that filches from me my good name
Robs me of that which not enriches him
And makes me poor indeed.

OTH.   By heaven, I 'll know thy thoughts.

IAGO.   You cannot, if my heart were in your hand;
Nor shall not, whilst 't is in my custody.

---

6. *leets*] days on which private jurisdiction courts were held.
7. *scattering*] random.

OTH.   Ha!
IAGO.   O, beware, my lord, of jealousy;
          It is the green-eyed monster, which doth mock
          The meat it feeds on: that cuckold lives in bliss
          Who, certain of his fate, loves not his wronger;[8]
          But, O, what damned minutes tells he o'er
          Who dotes, yet doubts, suspects, yet strongly loves!
OTH.   O misery!
IAGO.   Poor and content is rich, and rich enough;
          But riches fineless[9] is as poor as winter
          To him that ever fears he shall be poor:
          Good heaven, the souls of all my tribe defend
          From jealousy!
OTH.   Why, why is this?
          Think'st thou I 'ld make a life of jealousy,
          To follow still the changes of the moon
          With fresh suspicions? No; to be once in doubt
          Is once to be resolved: exchange me for a goat,
          When I shall turn the business of my soul
          To such exsufflicate[10] and blown surmises,
          Matching thy inference. 'T is not to make me jealous
          To say my wife is fair, feeds well, loves company,
          Is free of speech, sings, plays and dances well;
          Where virtue is, these are more virtuous:
          Nor from mine own weak merits will I draw
          The smallest fear or doubt of her revolt;
          For she had eyes, and chose me. No, Iago;
          I 'll see before I doubt; when I doubt, prove;
          And on the proof, there is no more but this,
          Away at once with love or jealousy!
IAGO.   I am glad of it; for now I shall have reason
          To show the love and duty that I bear you
          With franker spirit: therefore, as I am bound,
          Receive it from me. I speak not yet of proof.
          Look to your wife: observe her well with Cassio;
          Wear your eye thus, not jealous nor secure:
          I would not have your free and noble nature
          Out of self-bounty be abused; look to 't:
          I know our country disposition well;
          In Venice they do let heaven see the pranks

---

8. *his wronger*] his faithless wife.
9. *fineless*] endless.
10. *exsufflicate*] swollen like a bubble, inflated.

    They dare not show their husbands; their best conscience
    Is not to leave 't undone, but keep 't unknown.
OTH.   Dost thou say so?
IAGO.   She did deceive her father, marrying you;
    And when she seem'd to shake and fear your looks,
    She loved them most.
OTH.   And so she did.
IAGO.   Why, go to then;
    She that so young could give out such a seeming,
    To seel her father's eyes up close as oak — 11
    He thought 't was witchcraft — but I am much to blame;
    I humbly do beseech you of your pardon
    For too much loving you.
OTH.   I am bound to thee for ever.
IAGO.   I see this hath a little dash'd your spirits.
OTH.   Not a jot, not a jot.
IAGO.   I' faith, I fear it has.
    I hope you will consider what is spoke
    Comes from my love; but I do see you 're moved:
    I am to pray you not to strain my speech
    To grosser issues nor to larger reach
    Than to suspicion.
OTH.   I will not.
IAGO.   Should you do so, my lord,
    My speech should fall into such vile success
    As my thoughts aim not at. Cassio 's my worthy friend —
    My lord, I see you 're moved.
OTH.   No, not much moved:
    I do not think but Desdemona 's honest.
IAGO.   Long live she so! and long live you to think so!
OTH.   And yet, how nature erring from itself —
IAGO.   Ay, there 's the point: as — to be bold with you —
    Not to affect many proposed matches
    Of her own clime, complexion and degree,
    Whereto we see in all things nature tends —
    Foh! one may smell in such a will most rank,
    Foul disproportion, thoughts unnatural.
    But pardon me: I do not in position
    Distinctly speak of her; though I may fear
    Her will, recoiling to her better judgement,
    May fall to match you with her country forms,12

---

11. *close as oak*] close as the grain of oak.
12. *her country forms*] the form or outward aspect of her fellow-countrymen.

    And happily repent.

OTH.   Farewell, farewell:
    If more thou dost perceive, let me know more;
    Set on thy wife to observe: leave me, Iago.

IAGO.   [*Going*] My lord, I take my leave.

OTH.   Why did I marry? This honest creature doubtless
    Sees and knows more, much more, than he unfolds.

IAGO.   [*Returning*] My lord, I would I might entreat your honour
    To scan this thing no further; leave it to time:
    Though it be fit that Cassio have his place,
    For sure he fills it up with great ability,
    Yet, if you please to hold him off awhile,
    You shall by that perceive him and his means:
    Note if your lady strain his entertainment
    With any strong or vehement importunity;
    Much will be seen in that. In the mean time,
    Let me be thought too busy in my fears —
    As worthy cause I have to fear I am —
    And hold her free, I do beseech your honour.

OTH.   Fear not my government.[13]

IAGO.   I once more take my leave.   [*Exit.*]

OTH.   This fellow 's of exceeding honesty,
    And knows all qualities, with a learned spirit,
    Of human dealings. If I do prove her haggard,
    Though that her jesses[14] were my dear heart-strings,
    I 'ld whistle her off and let her down the wind
    To prey at fortune. Haply, for I am black
    And have not those soft parts of conversation
    That chamberers have, or for I am declined
    Into the vale of years, — yet that 's not much —
    She 's gone; I am abused, and my relief
    Must be to loathe her. O curse of marriage,
    That we can call these delicate creatures ours,
    And not their appetites! I had rather be a toad,
    And live upon the vapour of a dungeon,
    Than keep a corner in the thing I love
    For others' uses. Yet, 't is the plague of great ones;
    Prerogatived are they less than the base;
    'T is destiny unshunnable, like death:
    Even then this forked plague[15] is fated to us

---

13. *government*] self-control.
14. *haggard . . . jesses*] a wild or untrained hawk, "haggard," is sometimes used for "courtesan." "Jesses" are the leathern thongs which bind the hawk's foot to the falconer's wrist.
15. *forked plague*] a reference to the forked horns of a cuckolded husband.

When we do quicken.[16] Desdemona comes:

Re-enter DESDEMONA *and* EMILIA

    If she be false, O, then heaven mocks itself!
    I 'll not believe 't.
DES.   How now, my dear Othello!
    Your dinner, and the generous islanders
    By you invited, do attend your presence.
OTH.   I am to blame.
DES.   Why do you speak so faintly?
    Are you not well?
OTH.   I have a pain upon my forehead here.
DES.   Faith, that 's with watching; 't will away again:
    Let me but bind it hard, within this hour
    It will be well.
OTH.   Your napkin is too little;
       [He puts the handkerchief from him; and she drops it.]
    Let it alone. Come, I 'll go in with you.
DES.   I am very sorry that you are not well.
               [Exeunt OTHELLO *and* DESDEMONA.*]*
EMIL.   I am glad I have found this napkin:
    This was her first remembrance from the Moor:
    My wayward husband hath a hundred times
    Woo'd me to steal it; but she so loves the token,
    For he conjured her she should ever keep it,
    That she reserves it evermore about her
    To kiss and talk to. I 'll have the work ta'en out,[17]
    And give 't Iago: what he will do with it
    Heaven knows, not I;
    I nothing but to please his fantasy.

Re-enter IAGO

IAGO.   How now! what do you here alone?
EMIL.   Do not you chide; I have a thing for you.
IAGO.   A thing for me? it is a common thing —
EMIL.   Ha!
IAGO.   To have a foolish wife.
EMIL.   O, is that all? What will you give me now
    For that same handkerchief?

---

16. *When we do quicken*] When we are born.
17. *the work ta'en out*] the embroidery copied.

IAGO.   What handkerchief?
EMIL.   What handkerchief!
    Why, that the Moor first gave to Desdemona;
    That which so often you did bid me steal.
IAGO.   Hast stol'n it from her?
EMIL.   No, faith; she let it drop by negligence,
    And, to the advantage, I being here took 't up.
    Look, here it is.
IAGO.   A good wench; give it me.
EMIL.   What will you do with 't, that you have been so earnest
    To have me filch it?
IAGO.   [*Snatching it*] Why, what 's that to you?
EMIL.   If 't be not for some purpose of import,
    Give 't me again: poor lady, she 'll run mad
    When she shall lack it.
IAGO.   Be not acknown[18] on 't; I have use for it.
    Go, leave me.   [*Exit* EMILIA.]
    I will in Cassio's lodging lose this napkin,
    And let him find it. Trifles light as air
    Are to the jealous confirmations strong
    As proofs of holy writ: this may do something.
    The Moor already changes with my poison:
    Dangerous conceits are in their natures poisons,
    Which at the first are scarce found to distaste,
    But with a little act upon the blood
    Burn like the mines of sulphur. I did say so:
    Look, where he comes!

Re-enter OTHELLO

               Not poppy, nor mandragora,[19]
    Nor all the drowsy syrups of the world,
    Shall ever medicine thee to that sweet sleep
    Which thou owedst yesterday.
OTH.   Ha! ha! false to me?
IAGO.   Why, how now, general! no more of that.
OTH.   Avaunt! be gone! thou hast set me on the rack:
    I swear 't is better to be much abused
    Than but to know 't a little.
IAGO.   How now, my lord!
OTH.   What sense had I of her stol'n hours of lust?
    I saw 't not, thought it not, it harm'd not me:
    I slept the next night well, was free and merry;

---

18. *acknown*] knowing, acquainted with.
19. *mandragora*] an herb well known as a soporific or opiate.

    I found not Cassio's kisses on her lips:
    He that is robb'd, not wanting what is stol'n,
    Let him not know 't and he 's not robb'd at all.
IAGO.   I am sorry to hear this.
OTH.   I had been happy, if the general camp,
    Pioners and all, had tasted her sweet body,
    So I had nothing known. O, now for ever
    Farewell the tranquil mind! farewell content!
    Farewell the plumed troop and the big wars
    That make ambition virtue! O, farewell,
    Farewell the neighing steed and the shrill trump,
    The spirit-stirring drum, the ear-piercing fife,
    The royal banner and all quality,
    Pride, pomp and circumstance of glorious war!
    And, O you mortal engines, whose rude throats
    The immortal Jove's dread clamours counterfeit,
    Farewell! Othello's occupation 's gone!
IAGO.   Is 't possible, my lord?
OTH.   Villain, be sure thou prove my love a whore;
    Be sure of it; give me the ocular proof;
    Or, by the worth of man's eternal soul,
    Thou hadst been better have been born a dog
    Than answer my waked wrath!
IAGO.   Is 't come to this?
OTH.   Make me to see 't; or at the least so prove it,
    That the probation bear no hinge nor loop
    To hang a doubt on; or woe upon thy life!
IAGO.   My noble lord, —
OTH.   If thou dost slander her and torture me,
    Never pray more; abandon all remorse;
    On horror's head horrors accumulate;
    Do deeds to make heaven weep, all earth amazed;
    For nothing canst thou to damnation add
    Greater than that.
IAGO.   O grace! O heaven defend me!
    Are you a man? have you a soul or sense?
    God be wi' you; take mine office. O wretched fool,
    That livest to make thine honesty a vice!
    O monstrous world! Take note, take note, O world,
    To be direct and honest is not safe.
    I thank you for this profit, and from hence
    I 'll love no friend sith[20] love breeds such offence.

---

20. *sith*] since.

OTH. Nay, stay: thou shouldst be honest.
IAGO. I should be wise; for honesty 's a fool,
    And loses that it works for.
OTH.   By the world,
    I think my wife be honest, and think she is not;
    I think that thou art just, and think thou art not:
    I 'll have some proof. Her name, that was as fresh
    As Dian's visage, is now begrimed and black
    As mine own face. If there be cords, or knives,
    Poison, or fire, or suffocating streams,
    I 'll not endure it. Would I were satisfied!
IAGO. I see, sir, you are eaten up with passion:
    I do repent me that I put it to you.
    You would be satisfied?
OTH.   Would! nay, I will.
IAGO. And may: but, how? how satisfied, my lord?
    Would you, the supervisor,[21] grossly gape on?
    Behold her topp'd?
OTH.   Death and damnation! O!
IAGO. It were a tedious difficulty, I think,
    To bring them to that prospect: damn them then,
    If ever mortal eyes do see them bolster
    More than their own! What then? how then?
    What shall I say? Where 's satisfaction?
    It is impossible you should see this,
    Were they as prime as goats, as hot as monkeys,
    As salt as wolves in pride, and fools as gross
    As ignorance made drunk. But yet, I say,
    If imputation and strong circumstances,
    Which lead directly to the door of truth,
    Will give you satisfaction, you may have 't.
OTH. Give me a living reason she 's disloyal.
IAGO. I do not like the office:
    But sith I am enter'd in this cause so far,
    Prick'd to 't by foolish honesty and love,
    I will go on. I lay with Cassio lately,
    And being troubled with a raging tooth,
    I could not sleep.
    There are a kind of men so loose of soul,
    That in their sleeps will mutter their affairs:
    One of this kind is Cassio:
    In sleep I heard him say "Sweet Desdemona,

---

21. *supervisor*] onlooker.

Let us be wary, let us hide our loves;"
And then, sir, would he gripe and wring my hand,
Cry "O sweet creature!" and then kiss me hard,
As if he pluck'd up kisses by the roots,
That grew upon my lips: then laid his leg
Over my thigh, and sigh'd and kiss'd, and then
Cried "Cursed fate that gave thee to the Moor!"

OTH.   O monstrous! monstrous!
IAGO.   Nay, this was but his dream.
OTH.   But this denoted a foregone conclusion:
'T is a shrewd doubt, though it be but a dream.
IAGO.   And this may help to thicken other proofs
That do demonstrate thinly.
OTH.   I 'll tear her all to pieces.
IAGO.   Nay, but be wise: yet we see nothing done;
She may be honest yet. Tell me but this;
Have you not sometimes seen a handkerchief
Spotted[22] with strawberries in your wife's hand?
OTH.   I gave her such a one; 't was my first gift.
IAGO.   I know not that: but such a handkerchief—
I am sure it was your wife's — did I to-day
See Cassio wipe his beard with.
OTH.   If it be that, —
IAGO.   If it be that, or any that was hers,
It speaks against her with the other proofs.
OTH.   O, that the slave had forty thousand lives!
One is too poor, too weak for my revenge.
Now do I see 't is true. Look here, Iago;
All my fond love thus do I blow to heaven:
'T is gone.
Arise, black vengeance, from thy hollow cell!
Yield up, O love, thy crown and hearted throne
To tyrannous hate! Swell, bosom, with thy fraught,[23]
For 't is of aspics'[24] tongues!
IAGO.   Yet be content.
OTH.   O, blood, blood, blood!
IAGO.   Patience, I say; your mind perhaps may change.
OTH.   Never, Iago. Like to the Pontic sea,[25]

---

22. *Spotted*] Embroidered.
23. *fraught*] burden, freight.
24. *aspics*'] asps'.
25. *the Pontic sea*] the Pontic, now the Black sea, according to Pliny and the ancient geographers, had only a flowing tide, and never ebbed, for ever flowing into the Propontic, *i. e.*, the sea of Marmora, and the Hellespont, *i. e.*, the Bosphorus.

Whose icy current and compulsive course
Ne'er feels retiring ebb, but keeps due on
To the Propontic and the Hellespont;
Even so my bloody thoughts, with violent pace,
Shall ne'er look back, ne'er ebb to humble love,
Till that a capable and wide revenge
Swallow them up. Now, by yond marble heaven,
In the due reverence of a sacred vow   [*Kneels.*]
I here engage my words.

IAGO.   Do not rise yet.   [*Kneels.*]
Witness, you ever-burning lights above,
You elements that clip[26] us round about,
Witness that here Iago doth give up
The execution of his wit, hands, heart,
To wrong'd Othello's service! Let him command,
And to obey shall be in me remorse,
What bloody business ever.   [*They rise.*]

OTH.   I greet thy love,
Not with vain thanks, but with acceptance bounteous,
And will upon the instant put thee to 't:
Within these three days let me hear thee say
That Cassio 's not alive.

IAGO.   My friend is dead; 't is done at your request:
But let her live.

OTH.   Damn her, lewd minx! O, damn her!
Come, go with me apart; I will withdraw,
To furnish me with some swift means of death
For the fair devil. Now art thou my lieutenant.

IAGO.   I am your own for ever.   [*Exeunt.*]

SCENE IV. *Before the Castle.*

Enter DESDEMONA, EMILIA, *and* Clown

DES.   Do you know, sirrah, where Lieutenant Cassio lies?
CLO.   I dare not say he lies any where.
DES.   Why, man?
CLO.   He 's a soldier; and for one to say a soldier lies, is stabbing.

---

26. *clip*] embrace.

DES.   Go to: where lodges he?

CLO.   To tell you where he lodges, is to tell you where I lie.

DES.   Can any thing be made of this?

CLO.   I know not where he lodges; and for me to devise a lodging, and say he lies here or he lies there, were to lie in mine own throat.

DES.   Can you inquire him out and be edified by report?

CLO.   I will catechize the world for him; that is, make questions and by them answer.

DES.   Seek him, bid him come hither: tell him I have moved my lord on his behalf and hope all will be well.

CLO.   To do this is within the compass of man's wit, and therefore I will attempt the doing it.   [*Exit.*]

DES.   Where should I lose that handkerchief, Emilia?

EMIL.   I know not, madam.

DES.   Believe me, I had rather have lost my purse
Full of crusadoes:[1] and, but my noble Moor
Is true of mind and made of no such baseness
As jealous creatures are, it were enough
To put him to ill thinking.

EMIL.   Is he not jealous?

DES.   Who, he? I think the sun where he was born
Drew all such humours from him.

EMIL.   Look, where he comes.

DES.   I will not leave him now till Cassio
Be call'd to him.

Enter OTHELLO

                How is 't with you, my lord?

OTH.   Well, my good lady. [*Aside*] O, hardness to dissemble!
How do you, Desdemona?

DES.   Well, my good lord.

OTH.   Give me your hand: this hand is moist,[2] my lady.

DES.   It yet has felt no age nor known no sorrow.

OTH.   This argues fruitfulness and liberal heart:
Hot, hot, and moist: this hand of yours requires
A sequester from liberty, fasting and prayer,
Much castigation, exercise devout;
For here 's a young and sweating devil here,
That commonly rebels. 'T is a good hand,

---

1. *crusadoes*] gold coins of Portugal, marked with a cross.
2. *this hand is moist*] A moist hand was commonly held to be a sign of an amorous disposition, as a dry hand was held to be a sign of indifference to love.

A frank one.

DES.   You may, indeed, say so;
For 't was that hand that gave away my heart.

OTH. A liberal hand: the hearts of old gave hands;
But our new heraldry is hands, not hearts.

DES. I cannot speak of this. Come now, your promise.

OTH. What promise, chuck?

DES. I have sent to bid Cassio come speak with you.

OTH. I have a salt and sorry rheum offends me;
Lend me thy handkerchief.

DES. Here, my lord.

OTH. That which I gave you.

DES. I have it not about me.

OTH. Not?

DES. No, indeed, my lord.

OTH. That 's a fault. That handkerchief
Did an Egyptian[3] to my mother give;
She was a charmer,[4] and could almost read
The thoughts of people: she told her, while she kept it
'T would make her amiable and subdue my father
Entirely to her love, but if she lost it
Or made a gift of it, my father's eye
Should hold her loathed and his spirits should hunt
After new fancies: she dying gave it me,
And bid me, when my fate would have me wive,
To give it her. I did so: and take heed on 't;
Make it a darling like your precious eye;
To lose 't or give 't away were such perdition
As nothing else could match.

DES.   Is 't possible?

OTH. 'T is true: there 's magic in the web of it:
A sibyl,[5] that had number'd in the world
The sun to course two hundred compasses,
In her prophetic fury sew'd the work;
The worms were hallow'd that did breed the silk;
And it was dyed in mummy which the skilful
Conserved of maidens' hearts.

DES.   Indeed! is 't true?

OTH. Most veritable; therefore look to 't well.

DES. Then would to God that I had never seen 't!

---

3. *Egyptian*] Gypsy.
4. *charmer*] a practiser of enchantments, a witch.
5. *sibyl*] prophetess, sorceress.

OTH. Ha! wherefore?
DES. Why do you speak so startingly and rash?
OTH. Is 't lost? is 't gone? speak, is it out o' the way?
DES. Heaven bless us!
OTH. Say you?
DES. It is not lost; but what an if it were?
OTH. How!
DES. I say, it is not lost.
OTH. Fetch 't, let me see it.
DES. Why, so I can, sir, but I will not now.
      This is a trick to put me from my suit:
      Pray you, let Cassio be received again.
OTH. Fetch me the handkerchief: my mind misgives.
DES. Come, come;
      You 'll never meet a more sufficient man.
OTH. The handkerchief!
DES.   I pray, talk me of Cassio.
OTH. The handkerchief!
DES.   A man that all his time
      Hath founded his good fortunes on your love,
      Shared dangers with you, —
OTH. The handkerchief!
DES. In sooth, you are to blame.
OTH. Away!   [Exit.]
EMIL. Is not this man jealous?
DES. I ne'er saw this before.
      Sure there 's some wonder in this handkerchief:
      I am most unhappy in the loss of it.
EMIL. 'T is not a year or two shows us a man:
      They are all but stomachs and we all but food;
      They eat us hungerly, and when they are full
      They belch us. Look you, Cassio and my husband.

Enter CASSIO *and* IAGO

IAGO. There is no other way; 't is she must do 't:
      And, lo, the happiness! go and importune her.
DES. How now, good Cassio! what 's the news with you?
CAS. Madam, my former suit: I do beseech you
      That by your virtuous means I may again
      Exist, and be a member of his love
      Whom I with all the office of my heart
      Entirely honour: I would not be delay'd.
      If my offence be of such mortal kind,

That nor my service past nor present sorrows
Nor purposed merit in futurity
Can ransom me into his love again,
But to know so must be my benefit;
So shall I clothe me in a forced content
And shut myself up in some other course
To fortune's alms.

DES.   Alas, thrice-gentle Cassio!
My advocation is not now in tune;
My lord is not my lord, nor should I know him
Were he in favour as in humour alter'd.
So help me every spirit sanctified,
As I have spoken for you all my best
And stood within the blank of his displeasure
For my free speech! You must awhile be patient:
What I can do I will; and more I will
Than for myself I dare: let that suffice you.

IAGO.   Is my lord angry?

EMIL.   He went hence but now,
And certainly in strange unquietness.

IAGO.   Can he be angry? I have seen the cannon,
When it hath blown his ranks into the air,
And, like the devil, from his very arm
Puff'd his own brother; and can he be angry?
Something of moment then: I will go meet him:
There 's matter in 't indeed if he be angry.

DES.   I prithee, do so.   [*Exit* IAGO.]
                    Something sure of state,
Either from Venice or some unhatch'd practice
Made demonstrable here in Cyprus to him,
Hath puddled his clear spirit; and in such cases
Men's natures wrangle with inferior things,
Though great ones are their object. 'T is even so;
For let our finger ache, and it indues
Our other healthful members even to that sense
Of pain: nay, we must think men are not gods,
Nor of them look for such observancy
As fits the bridal. Beshrew me much, Emilia,
I was, unhandsome warrior as I am,
Arraigning his unkindness with my soul;
But now I find I had suborn'd the witness,
And he 's indicted falsely.

EMIL.   Pray heaven it be state-matters, as you think,
And no conception nor no jealous toy

Concerning you.
DES.   Alas the day, I never gave him cause!
EMIL.   But jealous souls will not be answer'd so;
    They are not ever jealous for the cause,
    But jealous for they are jealous: 't is a monster
    Begot upon itself, born on itself.
DES.   Heaven keep that monster from Othello's mind!
EMIL.   Lady, amen.
DES.   I will go seek him. Cassio, walk hereabout:
    If I do find him fit, I 'll move your suit,
    And seek to effect it to my uttermost.
CAS.   I humbly thank your ladyship.
                        [*Exeunt* DESDEMONA *and* EMILIA.]

Enter BIANCA

BIAN.   Save you, friend Cassio!
CAS.   What make you from home?
    How is it with you, my most fair Bianca?
    I' faith, sweet love, I was coming to your house.
BIAN.   And I was going to your lodging, Cassio.
    What, keep a week away? seven days and nights?
    Eight score eight hours? and lovers' absent hours,
    More tedious than the dial eight score times?
    O weary reckoning!
CAS.   Pardon me, Bianca:
    I have this while with leaden thoughts been press'd;
    But I shall in a more continuate time
    Strike off this score of absence. Sweet Bianca,
                 [*Giving her* DESDEMONA'S *handkerchief.*]
    Take me this work out.
BIAN.   O Cassio, whence came this?
    This is some token from a newer friend:
    To the felt absence now I feel a cause:
    Is 't come to this? Well, well.
CAS.   Go to, woman!
    Throw your vile guesses in the devil's teeth,
    From whence you have them. You are jealous now
    That this is from some mistress, some remembrance:
    No, by my faith, Bianca.
BIAN.   Why, whose is it?
CAS.   I know not, sweet: I found it in my chamber.
    I like the work well: ere it be demanded —
    As like enough it will — I 'ld have it copied:

Take it, and do 't; and leave me for this time.
BIAN.　　Leave you! wherefore?
CAS.　　I do attend here on the general;
　　And think it no addition, nor my wish,
　　To have him see me woman'd.
BIAN.　　　　　　　　　　　　　Why, I pray you?
CAS.　　Not that I love you not.
BIAN.　　　　　　　　　　　　But that you do not love me.
　　I pray you, bring me on the way a little;
　　And say if I shall see you soon at night.
CAS.　　'T is but a little way that I can bring you;
　　For I attend here: but I 'll see you soon.
BIAN.　　'T is very good; I must be circumstance.　　　　　*[Exeunt.]*

ACT IV.

SCENE I. *Cyprus. Before the Castle.*

Enter OTHELLO *and* IAGO

IAGO.　　Will you think so?
OTH.　　　　　　　　　　Think so, Iago!
IAGO.　　　　　　　　　　　　　　　What,
　　To kiss in private?
OTH.　　An unauthorized kiss.
IAGO.　　Or to be naked with her friend in bed
　　An hour or more, not meaning any harm?
OTH.　　Naked in bed, Iago, and not mean harm!
　　It is hypocrisy against the devil:
　　They that mean virtuously and yet do so,
　　The devil their virtue tempts and they tempt heaven.
IAGO.　　So they do nothing, 't is a venial slip:
　　But if I give my wife a handkerchief —
OTH.　　What then?
IAGO.　　Why, then, 't is hers, my lord; and being hers,
　　She may, I think, bestow 't on any man.
OTH.　　She is protectress of her honour too:
　　May she give that?
IAGO.　　Her honour is an essence that 's not seen:
　　They have it very oft that have it not:
　　But for the handkerchief —

OTH.   By heaven, I would most gladly have forgot it:
     Thou said'st — O, it comes o'er my memory,
     As doth the raven o'er the infected house,
     Boding to all — he had my handkerchief.
IAGO.   Ay, what of that?
OTH.   That 's not so good now.
IAGO.   What,
     If I had said I had seen him do you wrong?
     Or heard him say — as knaves be such abroad,
     Who having, by their own importunate suit,
     Or voluntary dotage of some mistress,
     Convinced or supplied them, cannot choose
     But they must blab —
OTH.   Hath he said any thing?
IAGO.   He hath, my lord; but be you well assured,
     No more than he 'll unswear.
OTH.   What hath he said?
IAGO.   Faith, that he did — I know not what he did.
OTH.   What? what?
IAGO.   Lie —
OTH.   With her?
IAGO.   With her, on her; what you will.
OTH.   Lie with her! lie on her! — We say lie on her, when they belie
     her. — Lie with her! 'Zounds, that's fulsome! Handker-
     chief — confessions — handkerchief! — To confess, and be
     hanged for his labour; first, to be hanged, and then to con-
     fess. I tremble at it. Nature would not invest herself in such
     shadowing passion without some instruction. It is not words that
     shakes me thus. Pish! Noses, ears and lips. Is 't possible? — Con-
     fess? — Handkerchief? — O devil!   [*Falls in a trance.*]
IAGO.   Work on,
     My medicine, work! Thus credulous fools are caught;
     And many worthy and chaste dames even thus,
     All guiltless, meet reproach. What, ho! my lord!
     My lord, I say! Othello!

Enter CASSIO

                How now, Cassio!
CAS.   What's the matter?
IAGO.   My lord is fall'n into an epilepsy:
     This is his second fit; he had one yesterday.
CAS.   Rub him about the temples.
IAGO.   No, forbear;

The lethargy must have his quiet course:
If not, he foams at mouth, and by and by
Breaks out to savage madness. Look, he stirs:
Do you withdraw yourself a little while,
He will recover straight: when he is gone,
I would on great occasion speak with you.   [*Exit* CASSIO.]
How is it, general? have you not hurt your head?

OTH.   Dost thou mock me?

IAGO.   I mock you! no, by heaven.
Would you would bear your fortune like a man!

OTH.   A horned man 's a monster and a beast.

IAGO.   There 's many a beast then in a populous city,
And many a civil monster.

OTH.   Did he confess it?

IAGO.   Good sir, be a man;
Think every bearded fellow that 's but yoked
May draw with you: there 's millions now alive
That nightly lie in those unproper beds
Which they dare swear peculiar: your case is better.
O, 't is the spite of hell, the fiend's arch-mock,
To lip[1] a wanton in a secure couch,
And to suppose her chaste! No, let me know;
And knowing what I am, I know what she shall be.

OTH.   O, thou art wise; 't is certain.

IAGO.   Stand you awhile apart;
Confine yourself but in a patient list.[2]
Whilst you were here o'erwhelmed with your grief —
A passion most unsuiting such a man —
Cassio came hither: I shifted him away,
And laid good 'scuse upon your ecstasy;
Bade him anon return and here speak with me;
The which he promised. Do but encave yourself,
And mark the fleers,[3] the gibes and notable scorns,
That dwell in every region of his face;
For I will make him tell the tale anew,
Where, how, how oft, how long ago and when
He hath and is again to cope your wife:
I say, but mark his gesture. Marry, patience;
Or I shall say you are all in all in spleen,
And nothing of a man.

---

1. *To lip*] To kiss.
2. *in a patient list*] within the bounds of patience.
3. *fleers*] sneers, looks of contempt.

OTH.   Dost thou hear, Iago?
I will be found most cunning in my patience;
But — dost thou hear? — most bloody.
IAGO.   That 's not amiss;
But yet keep time[4] in all. Will you withdraw?   [OTHELLO *retires*.]
Now will I question Cassio of Bianca,
A housewife[5] that by selling her desires
Buys herself bread and clothes: it is a creature
That dotes on Cassio; as 't is the strumpet's plague
To beguile many and be beguiled by one.
He, when he hears of her, cannot refrain
From the excess of laughter. Here he comes.

Re-enter CASSIO

As he shall smile, Othello shall go mad;
And his unbookish jealousy must construe
Poor Cassio's smiles, gestures and light behaviour,
Quite in the wrong. How do you now, lieutenant?
CAS.   The worser that you give me the addition[6]
Whose want even kills me.
IAGO.   Ply Desdemona well, and you are sure on 't.
Now, if this suit lay in Bianca's power,
How quickly should you speed!
CAS.   Alas, poor caitiff!
OTH.   Look, how he laughs already!
IAGO.   I never knew a woman love man so.
CAS.   Alas, poor rogue! I think, i' faith, she loves me.
OTH.   Now he denies it faintly and laughs it out.
IAGO.   Do you hear, Cassio?
OTH.   Now he importunes him
To tell it o'er: go to; well said, well said.
IAGO.   She gives it out that you shall marry her:
Do you intend it?
CAS.   Ha, ha, ha!
OTH.   Do you triumph, Roman? do you triumph?
CAS.   I marry her! what, a customer![7] I prithee, bear some charity to
my wit; do not think it so unwholesome. Ha, ha, ha!
OTH.   So, so, so, so: they laugh that win.

---

4. *keep time*] be patient; avoid haste.
5. *housewife*] used like "hussy."
6. *addition*] title.
7. *a customer*] a prostitute.

IAGO.   Faith, the cry goes that you shall marry her.

CAS.   Prithee, say true.

IAGO.   I am a very villain else.

OTH.   Have you scored me? Well.

CAS.   This is the monkey's own giving out: she is persuaded I will marry her, out of her own love and flattery, not out of my promise.

OTH.   Iago beckons me; now he begins the story.

CAS.   She was here even now: she haunts me in every place. I was the other day talking on the sea-bank with certain Venetians; and thither comes the bauble, and, by this hand, she falls me thus about my neck —

OTH.   Crying "O dear Cassio!" as it were: his gesture imports it.

CAS.   So hangs and lolls and weeps upon me; so hales and pulls me: ha, ha, ha!

OTH.   Now he tells how she plucked him to my chamber. O, I see that nose of yours, but not that dog I shall throw it to.

CAS.   Well, I must leave her company.

IAGO.   Before me! look, where she comes.

CAS.   'T is such another fitchew![8] marry, a perfumed one.

Enter BIANCA

What do you mean by this haunting of me?

BIAN.   Let the devil and his dam haunt you! What did you mean by that same handkerchief you gave me even now? I was a fine fool to take it. I must take out the work? A likely piece of work, that you should find it in your chamber, and not know who left it there! This is some minx's token, and I must take out the work? There; give it your hobby-horse:[9] wheresoever you had it, I 'll take out no work on 't.

CAS.   How now, my sweet Bianca! how now! how now!

OTH.   By heaven, that should be my handkerchief!

BIAN.   An you 'll come to supper to-night, you may; an you will not, come when you are next prepared for.   [*Exit.*]

IAGO.   After her, after her.

CAS.   Faith, I must; she 'll rail i' the street else.

IAGO.   Will you sup there?

CAS.   Faith, I intend so.

IAGO.   Well, I may chance to see you; for I would very fain speak with you.

CAS.   Prithee, come; will you?

---

8. *fitchew*] a polecat, a term commonly applied to a wanton woman.
9. *hobby-horse*] a term of contempt for a frivolous woman.

IAGO.   Go to; say no more.   [*Exit* CASSIO.]

OTH.   [*Advancing*] How shall I murder him, Iago?

IAGO.   Did you perceive how he laughed at his vice?

OTH.   O Iago!

IAGO.   And did you see the handkerchief?

OTH.   Was that mine?

IAGO.   Yours, by this hand: and to see how he prizes the foolish woman your wife! she gave it him, and he hath given it his whore.

OTH.   I would have him nine years a-killing. A fine woman! a fair woman! a sweet woman!

IAGO.   Nay, you must forget that.

OTH.   Ay, let her rot, and perish, and be damned to-night: for she shall not live: no, my heart is turned to stone; I strike it, and it hurts my hand. O, the world hath not a sweeter creature: she might lie by an emperor's side, and command him tasks.

IAGO.   Nay, that's not your way.

OTH.   Hang her! I do but say what she is: so delicate with her needle: an admirable musician: O, she will sing the savageness out of a bear: of so high and plenteous wit and invention: —

IAGO.   She's the worse for all this.

OTH.   O, a thousand thousand times: and then, of so gentle a condition!

IAGO.   Ay, too gentle.

OTH.   Nay, that's certain: but yet the pity of it, Iago! O Iago, the pity of it, Iago!

IAGO.   If you are so fond over her iniquity, give her patent[10] to offend; for, if it touch not you, it comes near nobody.

OTH.   I will chop her into messes: cuckold me!

IAGO.   O, 't is foul in her.

OTH.   With mine officer!

IAGO.   That's fouler.

OTH.   Get me some poison, Iago; this night. I 'll not expostulate with her, lest her body and beauty unprovide my mind again: this night, Iago.

IAGO.   Do it not with poison, strangle her in her bed, even the bed she hath contaminated.

OTH.   Good, good: the justice of it pleases: very good.

IAGO.   And for Cassio, let me be his undertaker:[11] you shall hear more by midnight.

---

10. *patent*] formal right, permission.
11. *let me . . . undertaker*] let me take up your cause of quarrel with him. "Undertaker" was the title commonly bestowed on such interveners in controversy.

OTH.   Excellent good. [*A trumpet within.*] What trumpet is that same?

IAGO.   Something from Venice, sure. 'T is Lodovico
Come from the duke: and, see, your wife is with him.

Enter LODOVICO, DESDEMONA, *and* Attendants

LOD.   God save the worthy general!

OTH.   With all my heart, sir.

LOD.   The duke and senators of Venice greet you.

[*Gives him a letter.*]

OTH.   I kiss the instrument of their pleasures.

[*Opens the letter, and reads.*]

DES.   And what 's the news, good cousin Lodovico?

IAGO.   I am very glad to see you, signior;
Welcome to Cyprus.

LOD.   I thank you. How does Lieutenant Cassio?

IAGO.   Lives, sir.

DES.   Cousin, there 's fall'n between him and my lord
An unkind breach: but you shall make all well.

OTH.   Are you sure of that?

DES.   My lord?

OTH.   [*Reads*] "This fail you not to do, as you will — "

LOD.   He did not call; he 's busy in the paper.
Is there division 'twixt my lord and Cassio?

DES.   A most unhappy one: I would do much
To atone them, for the love I bear to Cassio.

OTH.   Fire and brimstone!

DES.   My lord?

OTH.   Are you wise?

DES.   What, is he angry?

LOD.   May be the letter moved him;
For, as I think, they do command him home,
Deputing Cassio in his government.

DES.   By my troth, I am glad on 't.

OTH.   Indeed!

DES.   My lord?

OTH.   I am glad to see you mad.

DES.   Why, sweet Othello?

OTH.   Devil!   [*Striking her.*]

DES.   I have not deserved this.

LOD.   My lord, this would not be believed in Venice,
Though I should swear I saw 't: 't is very much:
Make her amends; she weeps.

OTH.   O devil, devil!
If that the earth could teem with woman's tears,

Each drop she falls would prove a crocodile.[12]
Out of my sight!
DES.   I will not stay to offend you.   [*Going.*]
LOD.   Truly, an obedient lady:
I do beseech your lordship, call her back.
OTH.   Mistress!
DES.   My lord?
OTH.   What would you with her, sir?
LOD.   Who, I, my lord?
OTH.   Ay; you did wish that I would make her turn:
Sir, she can turn and turn, and yet go on,
And turn again; and she can weep, sir, weep;
And she 's obedient, as you say, obedient,
Very obedient. Proceed you in your tears.
Concerning this, sir, — O well-painted passion! —
I am commanded home. Get you away;
I 'll send for you anon. Sir, I obey the mandate,
And will return to Venice. Hence, avaunt!   [*Exit* DESDEMONA.]
Cassio shall have my place. And, sir, to-night,
I do entreat that we may sup together:
You are welcome, sir, to Cyprus. Goats and monkeys!   [*Exit.*]
LOD.   Is this the noble Moor whom our full senate
Call all in all sufficient? This the nature
Whom passion could not shake? whose solid virtue
The shot of accident nor dart of chance
Could neither graze nor pierce?
IAGO.   He is much changed.
LOD.   Are his wits safe? is he not light of brain?
IAGO.   He 's that he is: I may not breathe my censure
What he might be: if what he might he is not,
I would to heaven he were!
LOD.   What, strike his wife!
IAGO.   Faith, that was not so well; yet would I knew
That stroke would prove the worst!
LOD.   Is it his use?
Or did the letters work upon his blood,
And new create this fault?
IAGO.   Alas, alas!
It is not honesty in me to speak
What I have seen and known. You shall observe him,
And his own courses will denote him so
That I may save my speech: do but go after,

---

12. *tears . . . crocodile*] Feigned tears are commonly known as "crocodile's tears."

And mark how he continues.

LOD.   I am sorry that I am deceived in him.   [*Exeunt.*]

SCENE II. *A Room in the Castle.*

Enter OTHELLO *and* EMILIA

OTH.   You have seen nothing, then?
EMIL.   Nor ever heard, nor ever did suspect.
OTH.   Yes, you have seen Cassio and she together.
EMIL.   But then I saw no harm, and then I heard
    Each syllable that breath made up between them.
OTH.   What, did they never whisper?
EMIL.   Never, my lord.
OTH.   Nor send you out o' the way?
EMIL.   Never.
OTH.   To fetch her fan, her gloves, her mask, nor nothing?
EMIL.   Never, my lord.
OTH.   That 's strange.
EMIL.   I durst, my lord, to wager she is honest,
    Lay down my soul at stake: if you think other,
    Remove your thought; it doth abuse your bosom.
    If any wretch have put this in your head,
    Let heaven requite it with the serpent's curse!
    For if she be not honest, chaste and true,
    There 's no man happy; the purest of their wives
    Is foul as slander.
OTH.   Bid her come hither: go.   [*Exit* EMILIA.]
    She says enough: yet she 's a simple bawd
    That cannot say as much. This is a subtle whore,
    A closet lock and key of villanous secrets:
    And yet she 'll kneel and pray; I have seen her do 't.

Enter DESDEMONA *with* EMILIA

DES.   My lord, what is your will?
OTH.   Pray, chuck, come hither.
DES.   What is your pleasure?
OTH.   Let me see your eyes;
    Look in my face.
DES.   What horrible fancy 's this?

OTH.   [*To* EMILIA] Some of your function, mistress,
     Leave procreants alone and shut the door;
     Cough, or cry hem, if any body come:
     Your mystery, your mystery: nay, dispatch.   [*Exit* EMILIA.]
DES.   Upon my knees, what doth your speech import?
     I understand a fury in your words,
     But not the words.
OTH.   Why, what art thou?
DES.   Your wife, my lord; your true and loyal wife.
OTH.   Come, swear it, damn thyself;
    Lest, being like one of heaven, the devils themselves
    Should fear to seize thee: therefore be double-damn'd;
    Swear thou art honest.
DES.   Heaven doth truly know it.
OTH.   Heaven truly knows that thou art false as hell.
DES.   To whom, my lord? with whom? how am I false?
OTH.   O Desdemona! Away! away! away!
DES.   Alas the heavy day! Why do you weep?
     Am I the motive of these tears, my lord?
     If haply you my father do suspect
     An instrument of this your calling back,
     Lay not your blame on me: if you have lost him,
     Why, I have lost him too.
OTH.   Had it pleased heaven
    To try me with affliction; had they rain'd
    All kinds of sores and shames on my bare head,
    Steep'd me in poverty to the very lips,
    Given to captivity me and my utmost hopes,
    I should have found in some place of my soul
    A drop of patience: but, alas, to make me
    A fixed figure for the time of scorn
    To point his slow unmoving finger at!
    Yet could I bear that too; well, very well:
    But there, where I have garner'd up my heart,
    Where either I must live or bear no life,
    The fountain from which my current runs,
    Or else dries up; to be discarded thence!
    Or keep it as a cistern for foul toads
    To knot and gender in! Turn thy complexion there,
    Patience, thou young and rose-lipp'd cherubin,
    Ay, there, look grim as hell!
DES.   I hope my noble lord esteems me honest.
OTH.   O, ay; as summer flies are in the shambles,
     That quicken even with blowing. O thou weed,

Who art so lovely fair and smell'st so sweet
That the sense aches at thee, would thou hadst ne'er been born!

DES.   Alas, what ignorant sin have I committed?

OTH.   Was this fair paper, this most goodly book,
Made to write "whore" upon? What committed!
Committed! O thou public commoner!
I should make very forges of my cheeks,
That would to cinders burn up modesty,
Did I but speak thy deeds. What committed!
Heaven stops the nose at it, and the moon winks;
The bawdy wind, that kisses all it meets,
Is hush'd within the hollow mine of earth,
And will not hear it. What committed!
Impudent strumpet!

DES.   By heaven, you do me wrong.

OTH.   Are not you a strumpet?

DES.   No, as I am a Christian:
If to preserve this vessel for my lord
From any other foul unlawful touch
Be not to be a strumpet, I am none.

OTH.   What, not a whore?

DES.   No, as I shall be saved.

OTH.   Is 't possible?

DES.   O, heaven forgive us!

OTH.   I cry you mercy then:
I took you for that cunning whore of Venice
That married with Othello. [*Raising his voice*] You, mistress,
That have the office opposite to Saint Peter,
And keep the gate of hell!

Re-enter EMILIA

                     You, you, ay, you!
We have done our course; there 's money for your pains:
I pray you, turn the key, and keep our counsel.   [*Exit.*]

EMIL.   Alas, what does this gentleman conceive?
How do you, madam? how do you, my good lady?

DES.   Faith, half asleep.

EMIL.   Good madam, what's the matter with my lord?

DES.   With who?

EMIL.   Why, with my lord, madam.

DES.   Who is thy lord?

EMIL.   He that is yours, sweet lady.

DES.   I have none: do not talk to me, Emilia;

I cannot weep, nor answer have I none
But what should go by water.[1] Prithee, to-night
Lay on my bed my wedding sheets: remember;
And call thy husband hither.
EMIL.   Here 's a change indeed!   [*Exit.*]
DES.   'T is meet I should be used so, very meet.
How have I been behaved, that he might stick
The small'st opinion on my least misuse?

Re-enter EMILIA *with* IAGO

IAGO.   What is your pleasure, madam? How is 't with you?
DES.   I cannot tell. Those that do teach young babes
Do it with gentle means and easy tasks:
He might have chid me so; for, in good faith,
I am a child to chiding.
IAGO.   What 's the matter, lady?
EMIL.   Alas, Iago, my lord hath so bewhored her,
Thrown such despite and heavy terms upon her,
As true hearts cannot bear.
DES.   Am I that name, Iago?
IAGO.   What name, fair lady?
DES.   Such as she says my lord did say I was.
EMIL.   He call'd her whore: a beggar in his drink
Could not have laid such terms upon his callet.[2]
IAGO.   Why did he so?
DES.   I do not know; I am sure I am none such.
IAGO.   Do not weep, do not weep. Alas the day!
EMIL.   Hath she forsook so many noble matches,
Her father and her country and her friends,
To be call'd whore? would it not make one weep?
DES.   It is my wretched fortune.
IAGO.   Beshrew him for 't!
How comes this trick upon him?
DES.   Nay, heaven doth know.
EMIL.   I will be hang'd, if some eternal villain,
Some busy and insinuating rogue,
Some cogging, cozening slave, to get some office,
Have not devised this slander; I 'll be hang'd else.
IAGO.   Fie, there is no such man; it is impossible.
DES.   If any such there be, heaven pardon him!

---

1. *go by water*] express itself in tears.
2. *callet*] a low prostitute.

EMIL.   A halter pardon him! and hell gnaw his bones!
    Why should he call her whore? who keeps her company?
    What place? what time? what form? what likelihood?
    The Moor 's abused by some most villanous knave,
    Some base notorious knave, some scurvy fellow.
    · O heaven, that such companions thou 'ldst unfold,
    And put in every honest hand a whip
    To lash the rascals naked through the world
    Even from the east to the west!
IAGO.   Speak within door.[3]
EMIL.   O, fie upon them! Some such squire he was
    That turn'd your wit the seamy side without,
    And made you to suspect me with the Moor.
IAGO.   You are a fool; go to.
DES.   O good Iago,
    What shall I do to win my lord again?
    Good friend, go to him; for, by this light of heaven,
    I know not how I lost him. Here I kneel:
    If e'er my will did trespass 'gainst his love
    Either in discourse of thought or actual deed,
    Or that mine eyes, mine ears, or any sense,
    Delighted them in any other form,
    Or that I do not yet, and ever did,
    And ever will, though he do shake me off
    To beggarly divorcement, love him dearly,
    Comfort forswear me! Unkindness may do much;
    And his unkindness may defeat my life,
    But never taint my love. I cannot say "whore":
    It doth abhor me now I speak the word;
    To do the act that might the addition earn
    Not the world's mass of vanity could make me.
IAGO.   I pray you, be content; 't is but his humour:
    The business of the state does him offence,
    And he does chide with you.
DES.   If 't were no other, —
IAGO.   'T is but so, I warrant.   [*Trumpets within.*]
    Hark, how these instruments summon to supper!
    The messengers of Venice stay the meat:
    Go in, and weep not; all things shall be well.
                        [*Exeunt* DESDEMONA *and* EMILIA.]

Enter RODERIGO

---

3. *Speak within door*] Don't speak so loud as to be heard outside the door.

How now, Roderigo!

ROD. I do not find that thou dealest justly with me.

IAGO. What in the contrary?

ROD. Every day thou daffest me with some device, Iago; and rather, as it seems to me now, keepest from me all conveniency than suppliest me with the least advantage of hope. I will indeed no longer endure it; nor am I yet persuaded to put up in peace what already I have foolishly suffered.

IAGO. Will you hear me, Roderigo?

ROD. Faith, I have heard too much; for your words and performances are no kin together.

IAGO. You charge me most unjustly.

ROD. With nought but truth. I have wasted myself out of my means. The jewels you have had from me to deliver to Desdemona would half have corrupted a votarist:[4] you have told me she hath received them and returned me expectations and comforts of sudden respect and acquaintance; but I find none.

IAGO. Well; go to; very well.

ROD. Very well! go to! I cannot go to, man; nor 't is not very well: by this hand, I say 't is very scurvy, and begin to find myself fopped in it.

IAGO. Very well.

ROD. I tell you 't is not very well. I will make myself known to Desdemona: if she will return me my jewels, I will give over my suit and repent my unlawful solicitation; if not, assure yourself I will seek satisfaction of you.

IAGO. You have said now.

ROD. Ay, and said nothing but what I protest intendment of doing.

IAGO. Why, now I see there 's mettle in thee; and even from this instant do build on thee a better opinion than ever before. Give me thy hand, Roderigo: thou hast taken against me a most just exception; but yet, I protest, I have dealt most directly in thy affair.

ROD. It hath not appeared.

IAGO. I grant indeed it hath not appeared, and your suspicion is not without wit and judgement. But, Roderigo, if thou hast that in thee indeed, which I have greater reason to believe now than ever, I mean purpose, courage and valour, this night show it: if thou the next night following enjoy not Desdemona, take me from this world with treachery and devise engines for my life.

ROD. Well, what is it? is it within reason and compass?

IAGO. Sir, there is especial commission come from Venice to depute Cassio in Othello's place.

---

4. *a votarist*] a nun.

ROD. Is that true? why then Othello and Desdemona return again to Venice.

IAGO. O, no; he goes into Mauritania, and takes away with him the fair Desdemona, unless his abode be lingered here by some accident: wherein none can be so determinate as the removing of Cassio.

ROD. How do you mean, removing of him?

IAGO. Why, by making him uncapable of Othello's place; knocking out his brains.

ROD. And that you would have me to do?

IAGO. Ay, if you dare do yourself a profit and a right. He sups to-night with a harlotry, and thither will I go to him: he knows not yet of his honourable fortune. If you will watch his going thence, which I will fashion to fall out between twelve and one, you may take him at your pleasure: I will be near to second your attempt, and he shall fall between us. Come, stand not amazed at it, but go along with me; I will show you such a necessity in his death that you shall think yourself bound to put it on him. It is now high supper-time, and the night grows to waste: about it.

ROD. I will hear further reason for this.

IAGO. And you shall be satisfied. [*Exeunt.*]

SCENE III. *Another Room in the Castle.*

Enter OTHELLO, LODOVICO, DESDEMONA, EMILIA, *and* Attendants

LOD. I do beseech you, sir, trouble yourself no further.

OTH. O, pardon me; 't will do me good to walk.

LOD. Madam, good night; I humbly thank your ladyship.

DES. Your honour is most welcome.

OTH.   Will you walk,[1] sir?

      O, — Desdemona, —

DES. My lord?

OTH. Get you to bed on the instant; I will be returned forthwith: dismiss your attendant there: look it be done.

DES. I will, my lord. [*Exeunt* OTHELLO, LODOVICO, *and* Attendants.]

EMIL. How goes it now? he looks gentler than he did.

DES. He says he will return incontinent:[2]

---

1. *walk*] withdraw.
2. *incontinent*] immediately.

     He hath commanded me to go to bed,
     And bade me to dismiss you.
EMIL.   Dismiss me!
DES.   It was his bidding; therefore, good Emilia,
     Give me my nightly wearing, and adieu:
     We must not now displease him.
EMIL.   I would you had never seen him!
DES.   So would not I: my love doth so approve him,
     That even his stubbornness, his checks, his frowns, —
     Prithee, unpin me, — have grace and favour in them.
EMIL.   I have laid those sheets you bade me on the bed.
DES.   All 's one. Good faith, how foolish are our minds!
     If I do die before thee, prithee, shroud me
     In one of those same sheets.
EMIL.   Come, come, you talk.
DES.   My mother had a maid call'd Barbara:
     She was in love; and he she loved proved mad
     And did forsake her: she had a song of "willow;"
     An old thing 't was, but it express'd her fortune,
     And she died singing it: that song to-night
     Will not go from my mind; I have much to do
     But to go hang my head all at one side
     And sing it like poor Barbara. Prithee, dispatch.
EMIL.   Shall I go fetch your night-gown?
DES.   No, unpin me here.
     This Lodovico is a proper man.
EMIL.   A very handsome man.
DES.   He speaks well.
EMIL.   I know a lady in Venice would have walked barefoot to Palestine
     for a touch of his nether lip.

DES.   [*Singing*]   The poor soul sat sighing by a sycamore tree,
           Sing all a green willow;
     Her hand on her bosom, her head on her knee,
           Sing willow, willow, willow:
     The fresh streams ran by her, and murmur'd her moans;
           Sing willow, willow, willow;
     Her salt tears fell from her, and soften'd the stones; —

     Lay by these: —

     [*Singing*]   Sing willow, willow, willow;

     Prithee, hie thee; he 'll come anon: —

     [*Singing*]   Sing all a green willow must be my garland.

Let nobody blame him; his scorn I approve, —

Nay, that's not next. Hark! who is 't that knocks?

EMIL.   It 's the wind.

DES.   [*Singing*]   I call'd my love false love; but what said he then?
   Sing willow, willow, willow:
 If I court moe[3] women, you 'll couch with moe men.

So get thee gone; good night. Mine eyes do itch;
Doth that bode weeping?

EMIL.   'T is neither here nor there.

DES.   I have heard it said so. O, these men, these men!
Dost thou in conscience think, — tell me, Emilia, —
That there be women do abuse their husbands
In such gross kind?

EMIL.   There be some such, no question.

DES.   Wouldst thou do such a deed for all the world?

EMIL.   Why, would not you?

DES.   No, by this heavenly light!

EMIL.   Nor I neither by this heavenly light; I might do 't as well i' the
dark.

DES.   Wouldst thou do such a deed for all the world?

EMIL.   The world 's a huge thing: it is a great price
For a small vice.

DES.   In troth, I think thou wouldst not.

EMIL.   In troth, I think I should; and undo 't when I had done. Marry,
I would not do such a thing for a joint-ring, nor for measures of
lawn, nor for gowns, petticoats, nor caps, nor any petty exhibition;[4] but, for the whole world, — why, who would not make her
husband a cuckold to make him a monarch? I should venture
purgatory for 't.

DES.   Beshrew me, if I would do such a wrong
For the whole world.

EMIL.   Why, the wrong is but a wrong i' the world; and having the world
for your labour, 't is a wrong in your own world, and you might
quickly make it right.

DES.   I do not think there is any such woman.

EMIL.   Yes, a dozen; and as many to the vantage[5] as would store the
world they played for.
But I do think it is their husbands' faults

---

3. *moe*] more.
4. *exhibition*] allowance.
5. *to the vantage*] into the bargain.

If wives do fall: say that they slack their duties
And pour our treasures into foreign laps,
Or else break out in peevish jealousies,
Throwing restraint upon us, or say they strike us,
Or scant our former having[6] in despite,
Why, we have galls, and though we have some grace,
Yet have we some revenge. Let husbands know
Their wives have sense[7] like them: they see and smell
And have their palates both for sweet and sour,
As husbands have. What is it that they do
When they change us for others? Is it sport?
I think it is: and doth affection breed it?
I think it doth: is 't frailty that thus errs?
It is so too: and have not we affections,
Desires for sport, and frailty, as men have?
Then let them use us well: else let them know,
The ills we do, their ills instruct us so.

DES.   Good night, good night: heaven me such uses send,
Not to pick bad from bad, but by bad mend!   [*Exeunt.*]

ACT V

SCENE I. *Cyprus. A Street.*

Enter IAGO *and* RODERIGO

IAGO.   Here, stand behind this bulk; straight will he come:
Wear thy good rapier bare, and put it home:
Quick, quick; fear nothing; I 'll be at thy elbow:
It makes us, or it mars us; think on that,
And fix most firm thy resolution.

ROD.   Be near at hand; I may miscarry in 't.

IAGO.   Here, at thy hand: be bold, and take thy stand. [*Retires.*]

ROD.   I have no great devotion to the deed;
And yet he hath given me satisfying reasons:
'T is but a man gone. Forth, my sword: he dies.

IAGO.   I have rubb'd this young quat[1] almost to the sense,

---

6. *having*] allowance for expenses.
7. *sense*] sensual appetite.
1. *quat*] pustule, pimple.

And he grows angry. Now, whether he kill Cassio,
Or Cassio him, or each do kill the other,
Every way makes my gain: live Roderigo,
He calls me to a restitution large
Of gold and jewels that I bobb'd[2] from him,
As gifts to Desdemona:
It must not be: if Cassio do remain,
He hath a daily beauty in his life
That makes me ugly; and besides, the Moor
May unfold me to him; there stand I in much peril:
No, he must die. Be 't so. I hear him coming.

Enter CASSIO

ROD.   I know his gait; 't is he. Villain, thou diest!
                                    [*Makes a pass at* CASSIO.]
CAS.   That thrust had been mine enemy indeed,
But that my coat is better than thou know'st:
I will make proof of thine.   [*Draws, and wounds* RODERIGO.]
ROD.   O, I am slain!
            [IAGO *from behind wounds* CASSIO *in the leg, and exit.*]
CAS.   I am maim'd for ever. Help, ho! murder! murder!   [*Falls.*]

Enter OTHELLO

OTH.   The voice of Cassio: Iago keeps his word.
ROD.   O, villain that I am!
OTH.   It is even so.
CAS.   O, help, ho! light! a surgeon!
OTH.   'T is he. O brave Iago, honest and just,
That hast such noble sense of thy friend's wrong!
Thou teachest me. Minion, your dear lies dead,
And your unblest fate hies: strumpet, I come!
Forth of my heart those charms, thine eyes, are blotted;
Thy bed lust-stain'd shall with lust's blood be spotted.   [*Exit.*]

Enter LODOVICO *and* GRATIANO

CAS.   What, ho! no watch? no passage?[3] murder! murder!
GRA.   'T is some mischance; the cry is very direful.
CAS.   O, help!

---

2. *bobb'd*] cheated or swindled.
3. *passage*] traffic, passersby.

LOD.   Hark!
ROD.   O wretched villain!
LOD.   Two or three groan: it is a heavy night:
     These may be counterfeits: let 's think 't unsafe
     To come in to the cry without more help.
ROD.   Nobody come? then shall I bleed to death.
LOD.   Hark!

Re-enter IAGO, *with a light*

GRA.   Here 's one comes in his shirt, with light and weapons.
IAGO.   Who 's there? whose noise is this that cries on murder?
LOD.   We do not know.
IAGO.   Did not you hear a cry?
CAS.   Here, here! for heaven's sake, help me!
IAGO.   What 's the matter?
GRA.   This is Othello's ancient, as I take it.
LOD.   The same indeed; a very valiant fellow.
IAGO.   What are you here that cry so grievously?
CAS.   Iago? O, I am spoil'd, undone by villains!
     Give me some help.
IAGO.   O me, lieutenant! what villains have done this?
CAS.   I think that one of them is hereabout,
     And cannot make away.
IAGO.   O treacherous villains!
     What are you there? come in and give some help.
                  [*To* LODOVICO *and* GRATIANO.]
ROD.   O, help me here!
CAS.   That 's one of them.
IAGO.   O murderous slave! O villain!
                        [*Stabs* RODERIGO.]
ROD.   O damn'd Iago! O inhuman dog!
IAGO.   Kill men i' the dark! Where be these bloody thieves?
     How silent is this town! Ho! murder! murder!
     What may you be? are you of good or evil?
LOD.   As you shall prove us, praise us.
IAGO.   Signior Lodovico?
LOD.   He, sir.
IAGO.   I cry you mercy. Here 's Cassio hurt by villains.
GRA.   Cassio!
IAGO.   How is 't, brother?
CAS.   My leg is cut in two.
IAGO.   Marry, heaven forbid!
     Light, gentlemen: I 'll bind it with my shirt.

Enter BIANCA

BIAN.   What is the matter, ho? who is 't that cried?
IAGO.   Who is 't that cried!
BIAN.   O my dear Cassio! my sweet Cassio! O Cassio, Cassio, Cassio!
IAGO.   O notable strumpet! Cassio, may you suspect
        Who they should be that have thus mangled you?
CAS.   No.
GRA.   I am sorry to find you thus: I have been to seek you.
IAGO.   Lend me a garter. So. O, for a chair,
        To bear him easily hence!
BIAN.   Alas, he faints! O Cassio, Cassio, Cassio!
IAGO.   Gentlemen all, I do suspect this trash
        To be a party in this injury.
        Patience awhile, good Cassio. Come, come;
        Lend me a light. Know we this face or no?
        Alas, my friend and my dear countryman
        Roderigo? no: — yes, sure: O heaven! Roderigo.
GRA.   What, of Venice?
IAGO.   Even he, sir: did you know him?
GRA.   Know him! ay.
IAGO.   Signior Gratiano? I cry you gentle pardon;
        These bloody accidents must excuse my manners,
        That so neglected you.
GRA.   I am glad to see you.
IAGO.   How do you, Cassio? O, a chair, a chair!
GRA.   Roderigo!
IAGO.   He, he, 't is he. [*A chair brought in.*] O, that 's well said; the chair:
        Some good man bear him carefully from hence;
        I 'll fetch the general's surgeon. [*To* BIANCA] For you, mistress,
        Save you your labour. He that lies slain here, Cassio,
        Was my dear friend: what malice was between you?
CAS.   None in the world; nor do I know the man.
IAGO.   [*To* BIAN.] What, look you pale? O, bear him out o' the
            air.   [CASSIO *and* RODERIGO *are borne off.*]
        Stay you, good gentlemen. Look you pale, mistress?
        Do you perceive the gastness⁴ of her eye?
        Nay, if you stare, we shall hear more anon.
        Behold her well; I pray you, look upon her:
        Do you see, gentlemen? nay, guiltiness will speak,
        Though tongues were out of use.

Enter EMILIA

_____

4. *gastness*] ghastliness, deadly paleness.

EMIL.   'Las, what's the matter? what's the matter, husband?
IAGO.   Cassio hath here been set on in the dark
    By Roderigo, and fellows that are 'scaped:
    He's almost slain, and Roderigo dead.
EMIL.   Alas, good gentleman! alas, good Cassio!
IAGO.   This is the fruit of whoring. Prithee, Emilia,
    Go know of Cassio where he supp'd to-night.
    What, do you shake at that?
BIAN.   He supp'd at my house; but I therefore shake not.
IAGO.   O, did he so? I charge you, go with me.
EMIL.   Fie, fie upon thee, strumpet!
BIAN.   I am no strumpet; but of life as honest
    As you that thus abuse me.
EMIL.   As I! foh! fie upon thee!
IAGO.   Kind gentlemen, let's go see poor Cassio dress'd.
    Come, mistress, you must tell 's another tale.
    Emilia, run you to the citadel,
    And tell my lord and lady what hath happ'd!
    Will you go on? I pray. [*Aside*] This is the night
    That either makes me or fordoes[5] me quite.   [*Exeunt.*]

SCENE II. A *Bedchamber in the Castle. Desdemona in Bed Asleep. A Light Burning.*

Enter OTHELLO

OTH.   It is the cause, it is the cause, my soul:
    Let me not name it to you, you chaste stars!
    It is the cause. Yet I'll not shed her blood,
    Nor scar that whiter skin of hers than snow
    And smooth as monumental alabaster.
    Yet she must die, else she'll betray more men.
    Put out the light, and then put out the light:
    If I quench thee, thou flaming minister,
    I can again thy former light restore,
    Should I repent me: but once put out thy light,
    Thou cunning'st pattern[1] of excelling nature,

---

5. *fordoes*] ruins, destroys.
1. *pattern*] model.

I know not where is that Promethean heat
That can thy light relume. When I have pluck'd the rose,
I cannot give it vital growth again,
It must needs wither: I 'll smell it on the tree.   [*Kissing her.*]
Ah, balmy breath, that dost almost persuade
Justice to break her sword! One more, one more:
Be thus when thou art dead, and I will kill thee,
And love thee after: one more, and this the last:
So sweet was ne'er so fatal. I must weep,
But they are cruel tears: this sorrow 's heavenly;
It strikes where it doth love. She wakes.

DES.   Who 's there? Othello?
OTH.   Ay, Desdemona.
DES.   Will you come to bed, my lord?
OTH.   Have you pray'd to-night, Desdemona?
DES.   Ay, my lord.
OTH.   If you bethink yourself of any crime
       Unreconciled as yet to heaven and grace,
       Solicit for it straight.
DES.   Alas, my lord, what may you mean by that?
OTH.   Well, do it, and be brief; I will walk by:
       I would not kill thy unprepared spirit;
       No; heaven forfend! I would not kill thy soul.
DES.   Talk you of killing?
OTH.   Ay, I do.
DES.   Then heaven have mercy on me!
OTH.   Amen, with all my heart!
DES.   If you say so, I hope you will not kill me.
OTH.   Hum!
DES.   And yet I fear you; for you are fatal then
       When your eyes roll so: why I should fear I know not,
       Since guiltiness I know not; but yet I feel I fear.
OTH.   Think on thy sins.
DES.   They are loves I bear to you.
OTH.   Ay, and for that thou diest.
DES.   That death 's unnatural that kills for loving.
       Alas, why gnaw you so your nether lip?
       Some bloody passion shakes your very frame:
       These are portents; but yet I hope, I hope,
       They do not point on me.
OTH.   Peace, and be still!
DES.   I will so. What 's the matter?
OTH.   That handkerchief which I so loved and gave thee
       Thou gavest to Cassio.

DES.   No, by my life and soul!
    Send for the man, and ask him.
OTH.   Sweet soul, take heed,
    Take heed of perjury; thou art on thy death-bed.
DES.   Ay, but not yet to die.
OTH.   Yes, presently:
    Therefore confess thee freely of thy sin;
    For to deny each article with oath
    Cannot remove nor choke the strong conception
    That I do groan withal. Thou art to die.
DES.   Then Lord have mercy on me!
OTH.   I say, amen.
DES.   And have you mercy too! I never did
    Offend you in my life; never loved Cassio
    But with such general warranty of heaven
    As I might love: I never gave him token.
OTH.   By heaven, I saw my handkerchief in 's hand.
    O perjured woman! thou dost stone my heart,
    And makest me call what I intend to do
    A murder, which I thought a sacrifice:
    I saw the handkerchief.
DES.   He found it then;
    I never gave it him: send for him hither;
    Let him confess a truth.
OTH.   He hath confess'd.
DES.   What, my lord?
OTH.   That he hath used thee.
DES.   How? unlawfully?
OTH.   Ay.
DES.   He will not say so.
OTH.   No, his mouth is stopp'd;
    Honest Iago hath ta'en order for 't.
DES.   O, my fear interprets! what, is he dead?
OTH.   Had all his hairs been lives, my great revenge
    Had stomach for them all.
DES.   Alas, he is betray'd, and I undone!
OTH.   Out, strumpet! weep'st thou for him to my face?
DES.   O, banish me, my lord, but kill me not!
OTH.   Down, strumpet!
DES.   Kill me to-morrow; let me live to-night!
OTH.   Nay, if you strive, —
DES.   But half an hour!
OTH.   Being done, there is no pause.
DES.   But while I say one prayer!

OTH. It is too late. [*He stifles her.*]

EMIL. [*Within*] My lord, my lord! what, ho! my lord, my lord!

OTH. What noise is this? Not dead? not yet quite dead?
    I that am cruel am yet merciful;
    ~~I would not have thee linger in thy pain:~~
    So, so.

EMIL. [*Within*] What, ho! my lord, my lord!

OTH. Who's there?

EMIL. [*Within*] O, good my lord, I would speak a word with you!

OTH. Yes: 't is Emilia. By and by. She 's dead.
    'T is like she comes to speak of Cassio's death.
    The noise was here. Ha! no more moving?
    Still as the grave. Shall she come in? were 't good?
    I think she stirs again. No. What 's best to do?
    If she come in, she 'll sure speak to my wife:
    My wife! my wife! what wife? I have no wife.
    O, insupportable! O heavy hour!
    Methinks it should be now a huge eclipse
    Of sun and moon, and that the affrighted globe
    Should yawn at alteration.

EMIL. [*Within*] I do beseech you
    That I may speak with you, O, good my lord!

OTH. I had forgot thee: O, come in, Emilia.
    Soft; by and by. Let me the curtains draw.
    Where art thou? [*Unlocks the door.*]

Enter EMILIA

    What's the matter with thee now?

EMIL. O, my good lord, yonder 's foul murders done!

OTH. What, now?

EMIL. But now, my lord.

OTH. It is the very error of the moon;
    She comes more nearer earth than she was wont
    And makes men mad.

EMIL. Cassio, my lord, hath kill'd a young Venetian
    Call'd Roderigo.

OTH. Roderigo kill'd!
    And Cassio kill'd!

EMIL. No, Cassio is not kill'd.

OTH. Not Cassio kill'd! then murder 's out of tune,
    And sweet revenge grows harsh.

DES. O, falsely, falsely murder'd!

EMIL. Alas, what cry is that?

OTH. That! what?
EMIL. Out, and alas! that was my lady's voice.
    Help! help, ho! help! O lady, speak again!
    Sweet Desdemona! O sweet mistress, speak!
DES. A guiltless death I die.
EMIL. O, who hath done this deed?
DES. Nobody; I myself. Farewell:
    Commend me to my kind lord: O, farewell!   [*Dies.*]
OTH. Why, how should she be murder'd?
EMIL.   Alas, who knows?
OTH. You heard her say herself, it was not I.
EMIL. She said so: I must needs report the truth.
OTH. She 's like a liar gone to burning hell:
    'T was I that kill'd her.
EMIL.   O, the more angel she,
    And you the blacker devil!
OTH. She turn'd to folly, and she was a whore.
EMIL. Thou dost belie her, and thou art a devil.
OTH. She was false as water.
EMIL.   Thou art rash as fire, to say
    That she was false: O, she was heavenly true!
OTH. Cassio did top her; ask thy husband else.
    O, I were damn'd beneath all depth in hell,
    But that I did proceed upon just grounds
    To this extremity. Thy husband knew it all.
EMIL. My husband!
OTH. Thy husband.
EMIL. That she was false to wedlock?
OTH. Ay, with Cassio. Nay, had she been true,
    If heaven would make me such another world
    Of one entire and perfect chrysolite,
    I 'ld not have sold her for it.
EMIL. My husband!
OTH.   Ay, 't was he that told me first:
    An honest man he is, and hates the slime
    That sticks on filthy deeds.
EMIL.   My husband!
OTH. What needs this iteration, woman? I say thy husband.
EMIL. O mistress, villany hath made mocks with love!
    My husband say that she was false!
OTH.   He, woman;
    I say thy husband: dost understand the word?
    My friend, thy husband, honest, honest Iago.
EMIL. If he say so, may his pernicious soul

Rot half a grain a day! he lies to the heart:
She was too fond of her most filthy bargain.

OTH.　Ha!

EMIL.　Do thy worst:
This deed of thine is no more worthy heaven
Than thou wast worthy her.

OTH.　　　　　　　　　　　　　　Peace, you were best.

EMIL.　Thou hast not half that power to do me harm
As I have to be hurt. O gull! O dolt!
As ignorant as dirt! thou hast done a deed —
I care not for thy sword; I 'll make thee known,
Though I lost twenty lives. Help! help, ho! help!
The Moor hath kill'd my mistress! Murder! murder!

Enter MONTANO, GRATIANO, IAGO, *and others*

MON.　What is the matter? How now, general!

EMIL.　O, are you come, Iago? you have done well,
That men must lay their murders on your neck.

GRA.　What is the matter?

EMIL.　Disprove this villain, if thou be'st a man:
He says thou told'st him that his wife was false:
I know thou didst not, thou 'rt not such a villain.
Speak, for my heart is full.

IAGO.　I told him what I thought, and told no more
Than what he found himself was apt and true.

EMIL.　But did you ever tell him she was false?

IAGO.　I did.

EMIL.　You told a lie, an odious, damned lie;
Upon my soul, a lie, a wicked lie!
She false with Cassio! Did you say with Cassio?

IAGO.　With Cassio, mistress. Go to, charm your tongue.

EMIL.　I will not charm my tongue; I am bound to speak:
My mistress here lies murder'd in her bed, —

ALL.　O heavens forfend!

EMIL.　And your reports have set the murder on.

OTH.　Nay, stare not, masters: it is true indeed.

GRA.　'T is a strange truth.

MON.　O monstrous act!

EMIL.　　　　　　　　　　　Villany, villany, villany!
I think upon 't: I think: I smell 't: O villany!
I thought so then: I 'll kill myself for grief:
O villany, villany!

IAGO.　What, are you mad? I charge you, get you home.

EMIL.   Good gentlemen, let me have leave to speak:
    'T is proper I obey him, but not now.
    Perchance, Iago, I will ne'er go home.
OTH.   O! O! O!   [*Falling on the bed.*]
EMIL.   Nay, lay thee down and roar;
    For thou hast kill'd the sweetest innocent
    That e'er did lift up eye.
OTH.   ·   [*Rising*]   O, she was foul!
    I scarce did know you, uncle: there lies your niece,
    Whose breath indeed these hands have newly stopp'd:
    I know this act shows horrible and grim.
GRA.   Poor Desdemona! I am glad thy father 's dead:
    Thy match was mortal to him, and pure grief
    Shore[2] his old thread in twain: did he live now,
    This sight would make him do a desperate turn,
    Yea, curse his better angel from his side,
    And fall to reprobation.
OTH.   'T is pitiful; but yet Iago knows
    That she with Cassio hath the act of shame
    A thousand times committed; Cassio confess'd it:
    And she did gratify his amorous works
    With that recognizance and pledge of love
    Which I first gave her; I saw it in his hand:
    It was a handkerchief, an antique token
    My father gave my mother.
EMIL.   O heaven! O heavenly powers!
IAGO.   'Zounds! hold your peace.
EMIL.   'T will out, 't will out. I peace!
    No, I will speak as liberal as the north:[3]
    Let heaven and men and devils, let them all,
    All, all, cry shame against me, yet I 'll speak.
IAGO.   Be wise, and get you home.
EMIL.   I will not.
               [IAGO *offers to stab* EMILIA.]
GRA.   Fie!
    Your sword upon a woman!
EMIL.   O thou dull Moor! that handkerchief thou speak'st of
    I found by fortune and did give my husband;
    For often with a solemn earnestness,
    More than indeed belong'd to such a trifle,
    He begg'd of me to steal it.

---

2. *Shore*] Cut.
3. *liberal as the north*] as free and as unrestrained as a blast of the north wind.

IAGO.   Villanous whore!

EMIL.   She give it Cassio! no, alas, I found it,
    And I did give 't my husband.

IAGO.   Filth, thou liest!

EMIL.   By heaven, I do not, I do not, gentlemen.
    O murderous coxcomb! what should such a fool
    Do with so good a wife?

OTH.   Are there no stones in heaven
    But what serve for the thunder? Precious villain!
        [*He runs at* IAGO: IAGO, *from behind, stabs* EMILIA, *and exit.*]

GRA.   The woman falls: sure, he hath kill'd his wife.

EMIL.   Ay, ay: O, lay me by my mistress' side.

GRA.   He 's gone, but his wife 's kill'd.

MON.   'T is a notorious villain. Take you this weapon,
    Which I have here recover'd from the Moor:
    Come, guard the door without; let him not pass,
    But kill him rather. I 'll after that same villain,
    For 't is a damned slave.   [*Exeunt all but* OTHELLO *and* EMILIA.]

OTH.   I am not valiant neither,
    But every puny whipster[4] gets my sword.
    But why should honour outlive honesty?
    Let it go all.

EMIL.   What did thy song bode, lady?
    Hark, canst thou hear me? I will play the swan,
    And die in music.   [*Singing*] Willow, willow, willow.
    Moor, she was chaste; she loved thee, cruel Moor;
    So come my soul to bliss, as I speak true;
    So speaking as I think, I die, I die.   [*Dies.*]

OTH.   I have another weapon in this chamber;
    It is a sword of Spain, the ice-brook's temper. — [5]
    O, here it is. Uncle, I must come forth.

GRA.   [*Within*] If thou attempt it, it will cost thee dear:
    Thou hast no weapon, and perforce must suffer.

OTH.   Look in upon me then, and speak with me,
    Or, naked[6] as I am, I will assault thee.

Re-enter GRATIANO

GRA.   What is the matter?

---

4. *whipster*] "whipper-snapper;" a term of contempt.
5. *a sword of Spain . . . temper*] The best swords came from Spain, and more especially
    from Bilboa or Toledo. The steel blades were tempered by plunging the steel while it
    was red-hot into ice-cold water.
6. *naked*] unarmed.

OTH.   Behold, I have a weapon;
     A better never did itself sustain
     Upon a soldier's thigh: I have seen the day
     That with this little arm and this good sword
     I have made my way through more impediments
     Than twenty times your stop:[7] but, O vain boast!
     Who can control his fate? 't is not so now.
     Be not afraid, though you do see me weapon'd;
     Here is my journey's end, here is my butt
     And very sea-mark of my utmost sail.
     Do you go back dismay'd? 't is a lost fear:
     Man but a rush against Othello's breast,
     And he retires. Where should Othello go?
     Now, how dost thou look now? O ill-starr'd wench!
     Pale as thy smock! when we shall meet at compt,[8]
     This look of thine will hurl my soul from heaven,
     And fiends will snatch at it. Cold, cold, my girl!
     Even like thy chastity. O cursed slave!
     Whip me, ye devils,
     From the possession of this heavenly sight!
     Blow me about in winds! roast me in sulphur!
     Wash me in steep-down gulfs of liquid fire!
     O Desdemona! Desdemona! dead!
     Oh! Oh! Oh!

Enter LODOVICO, MONTANO, CASSIO *carried in a chair, and* Officers *with*
IAGO, *prisoner*

LOD.   Where is this rash and most unfortunate man?
OTH.   That 's he that was Othello: here I am.
LOD.   Where is that viper? bring the villain forth.
OTH.   I look down towards his feet; but that 's a fable.[9]
     If that thou be'st a devil, I cannot kill thee.[10]   [*Wounds* IAGO.]
LOD.   Wrench his sword from him.
IAGO.   I bleed, sir, but not kill'd.
OTH.   I am not sorry neither: I 'ld have thee live;
     For, in my sense, 't is happiness to die.
LOD.   O thou Othello, that wert once so good,
     Fall'n in the practice of a damned slave,

---

   7. *your stop*] your power of resistance.
   8. *at compt*] at the day of reckoning or judgment.
   9. *I look down . . . fable*] a reference to the story that the Devil has cloven feet.
  10. *I cannot kill thee*] a reference to the belief that devils are immortal.

What shall be said to thee?

OTH.   Why, any thing:
An honourable murderer, if you will;
For nought did I in hate, but all in honour.

LOD.   This wretch hath part confess'd his villany:
Did you and he consent in Cassio's death?

OTH.   Ay.

CAS.   Dear general, I never gave you cause.

OTH.   I do believe it, and I ask your pardon.
Will you, I pray, demand that demi-devil
Why he hath thus ensnared my soul and body?

IAGO.   Demand me nothing; what you know, you know:
From this time forth I never will speak word.

LOD.   What, not to pray?

GRA.   Torments will ope your lips.

OTH.   Well, thou dost best.

LOD.   Sir, you shall understand what hath befall'n,
Which, as I think, you know not. Here is a letter
Found in the pocket of the slain Roderigo,
And here another: the one of them imports
The death of Cassio to be undertook
By Roderigo.

OTH.   O villain!

CAS.   Most heathenish and most gross!

LOD.   Now here's another discontented paper,
Found in his pocket too; and this, it seems,
Roderigo meant to have sent this damned villain;
But that, belike, Iago in the interim
Came in and satisfied him.

OTH.   O the pernicious caitiff!
How came you, Cassio, by that handkerchief
That was my wife's?

CAS.   I found it in my chamber:
And he himself confess'd but even now
That there he dropp'd it for a special purpose
Which wrought to his desire.

OTH.   O fool! fool! fool!

CAS.   There is besides in Roderigo's letter,
How he upbraids Iago, that he made him
Brave me upon the watch; whereon it came
That I was cast: and even but now he spake
After long seeming dead, Iago hurt him,
Iago set him on.

LOD.   You must forsake this room, and go with us:

      Your power and your command is taken off,
      And Cassio rules in Cyprus. For this slave,
      If there be any cunning cruelty
      That can torment him much and hold him long,
      It shall be his. You shall close prisoner rest,
      Till that the nature of your fault be known
      To the Venetian state. Come, bring away.
OTH.   Soft you; a word or two before you go.
      I have done the state some service, and they know 't.
      No more of that. I pray you, in your letters
      When you shall these unlucky deeds relate,
      Speak of me as I am; nothing extenuate,
      Nor set down aught in malice: then must you speak
      Of one that loved not wisely but too well;
      Of one not easily jealous, but, being wrought,
      Perplex'd in the extreme; of one whose hand,
      Like the base Indian, threw a pearl away
      Richer than all his tribe; of one whose subdued eyes,
      Albeit unused to the melting mood,
      Drop tears as fast as the Arabian trees
      Their medicinal gum. Set you down this;
      And say besides, that in Aleppo once,
      Where a malignant and a turban'd Turk
      Beat a Venetian and traduced the state,
      I took by the throat the circumcised dog
      And smote him, thus.   *[Stabs himself.]*
LOD.   O bloody period!
GRA.   All that 's spoke is marr'd.
OTH.   I kiss'd thee ere I kill'd thee: no way but this,
      Killing myself, to die upon a kiss.   *[Falls on the bed, and dies.]*
CAS.   This did I fear, but thought he had no weapon;
      For he was great of heart.
LOD.   *[To* IAGO*]*   O Spartan dog,
      More fell than anguish, hunger, or the sea!
      Look on the tragic loading of this bed;
      This is thy work: the object poisons sight;
      Let it be hid. Gratiano, keep the house,
      And seize upon the fortunes of the Moor,
      For they succeed on you. To you, lord governor,
      Remains the censure of this hellish villain,
      The time, the place, the torture: O, enforce it!
      Myself will straight aboard, and to the state
      This heavy act with heavy heart relate.   *[Exeunt.]*